SAVING CHARITY

EMMA ASHWOOD

PROLOGUE

Charity stood perfectly still in a brilliant white dress, holding a small posy of flowers.

Her mother, Glenda, looked radiant, her face enveloped in a broad smile.

She had a new dress for the occasion. What bride wouldn't? Even a widowed bride. Glenda's was blue and made by one of the finest tailors in New York City. It had cost a small fortune, but James had said she was worth it.

Charity looked from her mother to the man who just become her new stepfather. James McAllister. He was a huge man. He stood taller than her father and was twice as broad.

One thing that had struck Charity about James

since her mother had first introduced them was that he never seemed to smile very much.

Her father used to smile, laugh, and joke all the time. He used to say that he lived for laughter. Charity wasn't sure what James lived for, but she certainly knew it wasn't laughter.

She found it hard to believe that less than a year earlier she, her mother, her aunt, and her cousin had stood around her father's grave, watching his oak coffin being slowly lowered into the cold, snow-covered ground.

Charity had attended a few funerals in her time, and she noted how they always seemed to be held on a cold, wet, and miserable day. There was never anything to warm the heart at a funeral. She had hoped that she would never have to attend another one.

Her father's funeral service, held in the very church in which her mother was now being married, had been full. Charity's mother said it was a testament to how well-loved her father had been. Charity had taken comfort from that.

Today at the wedding, there was only a scattering of friends in attendance.

Charity wasn't sure of what to make of that. But she had her worries.

Her aunt, and therefore her cousin, had refused to attend the wedding because they didn't approve of James McAllister.

Charity wasn't sure why. She knew it couldn't just be because he didn't smile very much.

She'd heard heated arguments between the two sisters: her mother and Aunt Carol. She'd heard Aunt Carol shout, "It's too soon. You're leaping into this out of grief. You know what he is after."

Charity didn't really know what they were talking about. Her mother used to tell her by the firelight at night that women were meant to be married. They needed a man around the house to love and support them.

Charity just wished it could still be her father and not James.

But cholera had come to claim her father. Charity was just thirteen when it did. Her father was a merchant trader at the docks. An important man. But when cholera hit, it didn't discriminate. Her father was taken, just the same as it took the majority of his workers.

Now her mother had remarried, and a new stepfather would be moving into their home.

Despite the new dress and the posy of flowers, Charity wasn't happy about it all.

Five months later

Charity curled up in her bed and listened to the shouting coming from downstairs.

James was drunk. Again.

She did not recall her father ever drinking alcohol. Her stepfather never seemed to be without a glass in his hand.

When he got drunk, he got loud, and he often shouted at her mother. Once, he'd shouted at Charity but her mother soon put a stop to that.

She hated it when she heard the shouting from downstairs. More than once she knew her mother had been crying; she could hear her sobbing as she came upstairs to bed.

Charity was never sure what the arguments were about. Sometimes she heard the word money being spoken about and something about gambling.

She didn't even know what gambling was.

She was going to ask her mother but decided against it. If the word gambling made her mother's tears flow, then she wouldn't ask about it.

The next morning, she went downstairs and was shocked to see her mother with a bruise over her right eye.

"How did you get that?" Charity asked, instinctively reaching up and touching it gently with caring fingers.

"I fell over last night," her mother explained quickly. She winced as Charity's fingers explored the bruise.

"You need to be careful," Charity insisted.

"I was just being clumsy, that was all."

It was the first time Charity had seen her mother with a bruised face, but it wasn't the last.

The bruises always seem to appear after James had come home drunk and she heard shouting from downstairs. Her mother always insisted that they were caused by her falling over or having accidents.

Eventually, Charity put two and two together and realized that her stepfather was causing the bruises.

She wanted to ask her mother about it. She wanted to tell her to speak to Aunt Carol about it. But she knew it was pointless. To the best of her knowledge, her mother hadn't seen her sister or her niece since the day she married James.

Whenever she mentioned the bruises to her, her mother just clammed up and mentioned her clumsiness.

Charity once tried to say that she didn't like

James and didn't like the fact that he shouted all the time. But again, Glenda just shut her down, saying that James was a good man and that he was doing the best he could for them and how brave he was for taking on another man's child.

Charity wasn't sure about that. She wasn't sure about that at all.

Her father used to leave the house at 7 in the morning, after a quick breakfast of black coffee and dry toast. He would often not return until after six. Charity could see in his eyes how tired he was. Her stepfather was very different. James would lounge around in bed until mid-morning and then go to his club at lunchtime. She wasn't even sure what on earth he did by way of work.

She sometimes wondered if he didn't do anything at all.

Twelve months later

The bruises were still regularly seen on Glenda's face.

Once, Charity had happened upon her mother dressing and saw bruises all down her back and around her ribs.

"Why can't you be nice to my mother?" Charity finally snapped one afternoon.

James had been pestering Glenda regarding the

subject of money throughout the entire meal. He said he needed more, and Glenda said she didn't have it. He insisted that she had some hidden somewhere, which she denied. He raised his voice and called her some unsavory names.

Charity couldn't help it. The words just came out of her mouth. Fear danced in Glenda's eyes and she glanced across at her husband.

James slowly put down his teacup and glared at his stepdaughter. "I think you should go to your room until you learn some manners, girl."

Charity stared defiantly back at James for a moment before Glenda gently touched her on the knee.

"Do as your father says." It was a slip of the tongue. It was the first time Glenda had said it and she regretted it straight away.

"He isn't my father," Charity said in a surprisingly calm voice as she stood, turned, and fled to her bedroom.

Shouting soon erupted from down the stairs. Charity wasn't surprised to see her mother's face covered in bruises the following morning.

Charity felt nothing but guilt. She knew perfectly well that it was she who had caused her mother to be beaten that night. She wanted to tell her mother that they should throw James out of the house and tell him never to return. But she knew perfectly well that would not happen.

She knew she had to learn to endure her stepfather.

Six months later

"Why are they taking our furniture?" Charity demanded of her mother who stood motionless without responding. "Who are you?" Charity directed to one of the tall grim-faced men in their house when her mother didn't answer.

Three men dressed in black were lifting their belongings, carrying them outside, and loading them onto a cart.

Her mother was just as flustered. "Hush now, dear. Go upstairs."

James was nowhere to be seen. Strangely this had been one of the few days he had been awake and left the house early. He needed to be here to tell these men to go away.

Charity fled to her room and clutched her bible. It had been her father's. Her mother had given it to her shortly after he had died. It was nice to have it close; it gave her comfort, almost as if her father was close by.

She finally dared to venture back downstairs after she heard the door slam shut.

All the finest pieces of furniture are gone, leaving their beautiful house looking as if it had been ransacked.

"Why?" Charity started.

Her mother was sitting in the middle of the floor where the four huge red leather armchairs in which her father once sat used to be. Now they were gone.

"Because we owe some people some money. That's why," she answered.

"We?" Charity knew perfectly well that she didn't owe anyone any money and she was almost as sure that her mother owed no one money either. That just left her stepfather. Maybe this was part of the reason that some of their loyal hardworking staff had lost their jobs two months ago. Her mother had told her it was because they had been caught stealing. But she doubted it. If that were the case, they would have been replaced.

"Yes. We owe some money and the furniture will cover that debt."

"Where is James?" Charity asked. Her mother just looked vaguely at her. It was clear that she didn't know.

Worse was yet to come.

Two months later.

"Why have we got to move house?" Charity demanded.

"Please stop asking questions, Charity," her mother snapped a little too harshly.

She looked in the direction of her husband but was relieved that he hadn't heard her daughter's question.

"Because this house needs to be sold," she finally whispered under her breath when she realized Charity wasn't about to stop staring at her.

Charity was about to launch into another hundred questions, but James turned and joined them. Her mother simply shook her head at her daughter, warning her not to speak.

"I'm told it is comfortable enough," James said, somewhat unenthusiastically as he watched the cart disappear with their remaining furniture. "Once we get our bits in it."

Charity disagreed when she saw it. A tenement apartment.

She heard stories of the tenements and how horrific they were.

Life was hard and grim. Disease and poverty

were rampant. If cholera didn't kill you, then typhus would.

The buildings rose skyward in the rough areas of the city. They had narrow hallways with thin walls. Dirt and grime were everywhere. Rogue landlords ruled the corridors. They raised rents and plagued young widows with indecent proposals.

There were children everywhere. The families crammed into the tiny apartments seemed to have an endless brood of children. They spilled out into the hallways, stairs, and passageways, playing joyously and with smiles on their faces, as though they didn't understand the precarious positions in which they existed.

Peace was nowhere to be found hereabouts. Charity would not be able to read in the quiet solitude to which she had become accustomed.

They walked to their new abode. Glenda almost dying of shame during the walk. Charity was relieved to see that their tenement block was on the edge of the Lower East side. The further a person progressed into the area, the worse the buildings became.

The hallways and stairs seemed to have a fresh

lick of paint. The stairs didn't squeak and there was no smell of sewage.

The apartment was bigger than she expected. She heard horror stories of families of eight or more crammed into two rooms.

This tenement apartment had five rooms.

But it wasn't their beautiful home. It wasn't where she'd been born and where she had been brought up. It wasn't where she had memories of her beloved father.

As she settled down to sleep on that first night in the tenement, she wondered how much further they would have to fall.

One year later

With their servants gone, Glenda and Charity cooked and cleaned the apartment themselves.

It never bothered Charity. Strangely enough, she rather enjoyed scrubbing away dirt. It was as if she was scrubbing away the pain of the last few years.

It turned out that her mother was a marvelous cook. Where she learned the skill, Charity had no idea. Not that James was ever appreciative of their efforts. It was never good enough.

He had finally taken on work as a clerk in an insurance firm. However, he must've drank away half of his weekly salary. Every day he came home late, stinking of drink.

Her mother had taken on some small sewing jobs in order to bring in a few additional coins. From time to time, Charity helped her out but her needlework skills were never up to much.

Glenda promised Charity time after time that this wouldn't be forever. Charity couldn't see how life would ever be any different. They would never be able to regain everything they had lost.

One terrible day, news reached her mother that her sister Carol had died.

Her mother was full of regret that the two had not reconciled before Carol's death, and she was adamant that she would go to the funeral. A huge argument ensued on the matter between James and her. He said that Carol had never supported Glenda in her decision to marry James and that the woman was best dead and forgotten.

But Glenda was not going to be put off.

On that bleak and rainy day, Charity and her mother made their way to the cemetery.

Clara May, Aunt Carol's daughter and Charity's cousin, welcomed them with an open heart. She told Glenda that her mother's death had proved to actually be somewhat of a mercy in the end. It was probably cancer of the stomach that had killed her. Over the previous six months, Carol had wasted away to almost nothing.

Clara was six years older than Charity and the two became firm friends.

Charity would visit her cousin weekly. Following the death of Aunt Carol, Clara had inherited everything. She would not need to cook or clean for herself.

Charity sometimes felt a little ashamed about her own situation. When she visited, she would always wear the same dress and keep the topic of conversation firmly away from her life. Clara was a source of inspiration to Charity who was amazed at how well she had coped after the death of Aunt Carol. Charity knew that her aunt would have been proud of her and hoped that if anything ever happened to her mother, she would be the same.

Unfortunately, she got to find out firsthand sooner rather than later.

Four months later

Influenza ripped through the tenements of the Lower East side quicker than a raging fire.

Despite its position on the edge and being better than most, their building wasn't spared. All three of them were struck down with the illness, leaving them weak and helpless.

They had fevers for what seemed like days, a cough that rattled their chests, and fitful sleep that was plagued with nightmares.

James and Charity slowly recovered.

Glenda did not. Her skin grew grey and clammy. Her breathing slower and shallow. Charity watched in horror as her mother slipped away.

She could do nothing to prevent it.

As she held her mother's lifeless hand, she realized that she was now alone and at the mercy of her stepfather,

CHAPTER 1

Eighteen Months Later

"Charity?" the burly man called as he walked into the tenement in New York City. The man was obviously drunk. The only thing on his mind as he stumbled home through the dark city streets that night was giving his stepdaughter a talking-to.

Charity Bryant was sitting up in bed, visibly shaking in her nightgown as she heard him move from room to room. This wasn't the first time he had come home drunk, but he would usually simply stumble to his bedroom across the hall and that was that. Sadly, this night didn't seem to be going that way. Charity edged toward the door, her father's bible in her hand, and peeked through the crack to see her stepfather, James, battling to get his shoes off. He was squeezed on the tiny wooden bench that Charity's mother, Glenda, had placed against the wall. During the struggle, he fell and landed on his back on the rough wooden floor.

He yelled in disgust and Charity grew even more frightened.

She hugged the book closer to her chest, hoping it would provide her some comfort, but there was nothing comfortable about this situation. Charity had the sneaking suspicion that as soon as her stepfather found his footing, he would be heading directly to her. And there was nowhere for her to run. They were eight floors up in the tenement building, leaving Charity only the option of hiding under her bed. But that was an idea, at least. Perhaps her stepfather would get sick of looking for her and retire to his own bedroom before he noticed that his stepdaughter was curled up under her cot, the sheer bed curtains hiding her stark white face.

Just as Charity was edging from the door to the bed, the door burst open. It seemed that her stepfather had found his footing.

"Come here, you horrible girl!" he shouted, grabbing Charity roughly by the arm and bringing her close to him. He didn't stop until her face was mere inches from his. His breath stank of drink and it made her feel sick. "Now you listen here, and you listen good, my girl. I won't stand for the way you've been handling this house and the way you have been treating me. You're all I've got left in this world now that your mother is gone, and I expect you to fill her shoes, you hear? My dinner's been cold the last three nights, my bed hasn't been made, and the place is filthy. If you want to stay here, you have to earn your keep, you hear? You ain't my daughter. Remember that. You are here by my good grace."

Spittle flew from her stepfather's mouth, landing on Charity's face. She tried to lean away and made an attempt to free herself from his vice-like grip, but he sensed her need to escape and only held her all the tighter. Charity could feel the bruise beginning to form on her arm. She would have to hide it under long sleeves tomorrow, which would look so odd in the heat of the city summer.

"Yes, sir. I understand," Charity whispered, hoping it would appease him. There was no real truth in what he said. His dinner had been cold because he had arrived late after going out drinking. The place was always clean until he arrived home and made an unholy mess every night. Even his bed was made until he fell into it and caused it to appear unkempt.

"You look me in the eye when you're talking to me, girl," he snarled at her.

Charity nodded and looked up. "Yes, sir. I understand what you say. Completely. I'll do better." She knew there was no point in arguing. It was a lesson her mother had quickly learned after the wedding.

He released her, and Charity fell back against her bed, her bible still clutched tightly in her hand.

"I'm going to sleep, but if I wake up tomorrow and my breakfast isn't on the table, mark my words, there will be punishment. Your mother isn't here to make excuses for you anymore, Charity."

Charity watched him walk away and when she was sure his door had been shut, she quickly closed her own, wishing not for the first time that hers had a lock. She crawled back under the covers and opened the bible to the chapter of the Gospel of Mark that she had been reading, hoping the Lord's words would give her comfort. Tears dropped from her eyes to the thin paper pages as she read.

At least she had Clayton, she thought.

Soon she'd be far away from this place, out West with a man who wouldn't intimidate her or make her feel worthless. She drifted off to sleep with visions dancing in her head of weddings and a happy life on a ranch in a faraway place called Texas.

The most wonderful thing about it was that James didn't know a thing about it.

"You can't be serious?" Charity's cousin Clara May said the next day while pouring tea from an old, chipped blue teapot. "It's preposterous! You can't simply leave New York to marry a man you've never met who lives five days' travel from all you do know!"

"I not only can but I will. I have to get out of that place, Clara. You don't understand. He's so awful. I start shaking with fear when he gets within a few feet of me. It's no way to live. He... he beats me, Clara. Just like he used to beat my mother. He beats me and he's always drunk and I'm afraid that one night, he's going to come home and do a great deal worse than just beating me."

Clara looked shocked by this revelation. She knew Charity's stepfather was a highly unpleasant man. She had wished that her Aunt Glenda hadn't married him. It was criminal how he had managed to squander away her money. Her own mother had warned her, but it had simply led to a falling out between the two sisters. Despite her knowledge of his character, she had no idea that he was beating Charity. She put down the teapot and reached across the linen tablecloth to take her cousin's hand in hers. "I'm so sorry. I wish you'd told me sooner. Why don't you just come live here? It is the obvious solution. There's more than enough room, and I'd easily be able to support you. You wouldn't have to do anyone's washing or cooking. You could finally give yourself the chance to heal after your mother's death. And you'd be safe here. No one would hurt you. I promise you that."

Charity smiled sadly and looked into her cup of tea. She picked up the jug of milk and added a drop and then a sugar cube, and stirred idly while she pondered. As much as she loved the idea of living with Clara—she was, after all, not just her cousin, but also her best friend—living with her would also mean staying in New York City. She wanted desperately to escape the city and its memories. It was those memories of happier times that hurt the most. He would always be lurking in the background. She could never walk down the street and not know that he was there. Charity wanted a new life.

"As wonderful as that sounds, it's not enough. I can't just move to a different house. I need to get away from him entirely. Did you know that he was trying to marry me off to his brother? The man is fifty years old if he's a day and is a worse drunk than him, if such a thing was possible. And besides, I want to marry Clayton. He's a good, honest man, Clara. Here, look at some of the letters he sent me." Charity got up and went to her reticule, which she had laid on the table near the stove. She took out a bundle of letters secured with a ribbon and brought them back to Clara.

"Here, read some. You'll see," she said, handing the letters over to Clara. "I've been corresponding with him for months."

Clara flicked through them, noting the accomplished hand and the reverent way in which he addressed her cousin, using terms of endearment such as "cherished love" and "darling." She had rather imagined a cowboy to be rough and with little education. It seemed that the man Clara intended to marry was more than just that.

"They're all like that," Charity said when Clara reached for the last of the letters. "From the moment I first started corresponding with him, he's been so warm and kind. And I won't just be moving in with him. His older brother Edrick lives with him as well, so we'll be like a little family. Edrick lost his wife, you see, so now Clayton is the only family he has." Clara didn't seem convinced, so Charity pressed on. "I'm not the first woman to do this, you know! Far from it. Hundreds, perhaps thousands of women have answered mail-order bride advertisements and headed west to marry men they've never met. I think it'll be good for me, Clara. A fresh start with a loving husband and plenty of fresh air. It's what I want."

"I simply don't think it's a good idea, Charity. Who's to say this man isn't simply posturing in his letters, and when you get there you won't be met by some vicious ogre who treats you poorly and beats you? He might not even live on a ranch. And you'll be stuck far away from me or anyone else who could help you! You'll be going from one problem to the next. You're just nineteen years of age. You're beautiful. You will have suitors falling at your feet. But you are going to head west to marry a man you have never laid eyes on. Charity, you must see the problems you are going to cause yourself." Clara settled back into her chair and eyed Charity carefully.

Tears sprang to Charity's eyes at her cousin's harsh words. She knew they held a grain of truth and that for all she knew, Clayton could turn out to be even worse than her stepfather. But she hoped and prayed that he was the man he had made himself out to be in his letters. She needed this, a new life, a new home, a new companion. She was depending on it.

She decided to say as much to her cousin. "Please, Clara. I...I can't stay in New York any longer. It's too painful, what with Father and Mother. I would never feel safe with my stepfather still in the city. You know as well as I do that he won't like me just leaving. If he ever cast eyes on me again," she paused and looked Clara dead in the eye. "I dread to think what he would do. It's just too much. I need to start over. I need..." but she couldn't finish her sentence. Sobs began to wrack her body, and soon she was doubled over in her chair, letting her tears drop onto her grey dress and holding herself in a tightly wrapped ball. Clara was out of her seat and at her cousin's side in a flash.

"Oh Charity, please don't cry. I just can't bear to

see you hurt again, and I'm afraid this new man, this Clayton, will hurt you. I just can't permit you to go. Unless…" Clara paused, considering an idea that was at once brash and also somehow made perfect sense. "Unless I can go with you. How's that? I'll take the train with you and we can journey west together. I'll return when I see you safely settled."

Charity looked up at Clara and nodded. "Yes. Yes. What a wonderful idea! An adventure together. Oh, Clara, thank you," she cried and wrapped her arms around her cousin and hugged her tight. Clara hoped she had made the right decision. She couldn't resist the urge to help her best friend and only cousin. She couldn't stand to see her stuck in a city that had caused her so much grief and pain.

CHAPTER 2

As Clara meticulously packed her modest trunk for the impending train journey she had booked for herself and Charity, a wave of unadulterated panic washed over her. She had never before set foot on a train, never ventured outside the bustling confines of New York City, and had never even entertained the notion of traveling until she had impulsively declared to Charity that she would accompany her all the way to Texas.

At the age of twenty-five, Clara came to the startling realization that she knew precious little about the world beyond the concrete jungle of New York. Indeed, her knowledge barely extended beyond the comfortable, familiar sphere of her own social circle. She hadn't even once visited the tenement that Charity now begrudgingly called home. Naturally, that was due to James' adamant refusal to allow it, of course.

Is this all a grave mistake? Clara pondered to herself as she carefully nestled her petite jewelry box beneath the folds of her three finest dresses. After all, what on Earth had possessed her to embark on such a journey to the untamed West so that Charity could wed a man she'd never even laid eyes on? And to live on a sprawling ranch? Clara had never so much as glimpsed a real, live cow! The mere sight of the horses that dutifully pulled the carriages she rode in when traversing the city was nearly too much for her to bear. True, the ranch primarily raised cattle, but she had no doubt that horses would be the primary mode of transportation. The horrifying thought of having to ride one of those beasts--and what if she were to lose her balance and fall to her death?

Deep, calming breaths, Clara instructed herself as she secured the well-worn trunk and retreated to sit down on her plush bed. Though the plan was undoubtedly unconventional, she couldn't simply stand idly by and watch her beloved cousin journey to some distant, unknown place to marry a stranger without thoroughly assessing his character. Clara needed to be there, to ensure Charity's safety and wellbeing. And if that meant venturing into the wilds of the West, then so be it. She would do anything--even risk her own life--for her best friend and cherished cousin. As Charity's sole remaining family, Clara felt a profound sense of duty.

That, however, didn't mean she would abandon all reason.

Clara had firmly insisted that Charity write to Clayton and ascertain that proper arrangements would be made for their arrival. She also pressed the matter of finding a suitable chaperone to accompany them until the day of Charity's wedding, although Clara harbored little hope in that regard. Would there even be any other women on the ranch? She could only speculate. Moreover, she wanted the wedding to be postponed until the couple had ample time to become better acquainted, rather than marrying on the very day of her arrival, as initially planned.

"Just because you've exchanged letters with him doesn't mean he can't be a confidence trickster," Clara had reasoned. Her cousin surely couldn't marry the man until she truly knew him, understood how he ran his ranch and managed his household. Only then could Charity determine whether he was a man worthy of pledging her life to.

Charity had been less than thrilled with this proposal. However, in the end, she had begrudgingly acquiesced once Clara had made it abundantly clear that she would refuse to accompany her to Texas unless she knew that Charity wouldn't marry Clayton until she felt entirely ready.

"Clara, my dearest, you do know that my Clayton is not at all the sort of man you suspect him to be. A confidence trickster, indeed," she had huffed. "That dastardly fellow whom the Gazette and New York Herald dubbed the 'confidence man', Samuel Thompson, has been securely locked away in prison since July 1849 after duping so many unsuspecting souls. He was quite the bungling swindler, too. Clayton will not ensnare me as a victim gained through misplaced confidence, I assure you."

Clara was impressed that Charity had drawn a connection to the incarcerated Thompson. Perhaps Charity was more worldly and astute than her cousin had initially realized.

Regardless, now that both the packing and the wedding postponement had been addressed, Clara had one final task to attend to. She had already informed her manager at the tailor shop that she wouldn't be returning after her Saturday shift. Even if she did come back, she couldn't expect him to hold her position indefinitely. She had instructed him to offer it to someone truly in need. Clara's work at the shop was limited to three days a week, and her reasons for working were more for camaraderie and a sense of purpose than any financial necessity. Now, all that remained was for her to consult her lawyer. She donned her elegant cape and informed her maid that she wouldn't be back until supper, and then she made her way to Seymour & Sons in the heart of downtown Manhattan.

Seymour & Sons had managed Clara's legal affairs since her mother's untimely death and her subsequent inheritance. Prior to that, her father had been a loyal client of the firm. They had also represented Charity's father before his own demise. The firm had advised Glenda that marrying James would be a disastrous decision, and their prediction had been tragically accurate. Eric Seymour had become somewhat of a father figure to Clara, dispensing advice and suggestions as he deemed appropriate. And today was no exception. Clara sat before the distinguished older gentleman, his glasses perched upon his nose and a cup of tepid tea before him, as he vehemently insisted that her plan was simply preposterous.

"Moving to Texas? To live with two men you don't even know? Come now, Miss Clara, you're an intelligent young woman. You can't genuinely believe this to be a sound decision. Anything could happen out there. It's called the Wild West for a reason, my dear girl!"

"I'm well aware, Mr. Seymour, but I'm doing this for Charity. She has endured such hardships. You know all too well, with her father passing in such a manner and her mother being beguiled by that scoundrel. Now her mother is gone, and she has nothing left here. She's convinced that her only path forward is to flee New York City and seek a new life out West. I must accompany her, to ensure her safety. It's my duty as her best friend and sole cousin. And once she's settled, we will evaluate the best options for my own future. Perhaps the West will prove a sensible choice for me to establish myself, rather than returning here. I am keeping my options open."

Eric Seymour had offered Clara some sage advice when she had come into her inheritance. He cautioned her to be wary of men, pointing out how her Aunt Glenda had married the dashing but ultimately disastrous James, who had squandered everything her first husband had painstakingly built. He had warned Clara that she would encounter no shortage of suitors vying for her hand and that she must exercise great caution. She had taken that advice to heart, and perhaps that was why she remained unwed at twenty-five.

Mr. Seymour took a tentative sip of his tea, grimaced at the taste, then set it down and folded his hands beneath his chin. "Well, if that's how you feel, then I cannot dissuade you. You're a grown woman. You can make your own decisions, Miss Clara. All I ask is that you write to me and keep me informed of your well-being."

"I will, of course, Mr. Seymour. I may very well return as soon as Charity is wed. Nevertheless, there is a matter I wanted to discuss with you before I depart," Clara said. She had been nervously wringing her hands in her lap, but now she laid them flat on the desk before her and leaned in. "Mr. Seymour, I would like you to help me draft my will."

Mr. Seymour sat up straight in his chair and looked shocked. "Miss Clara! I was only jesting about that Wild West business. Matters have calmed down considerably out there, or so I've heard. I'm certain you'll be just fine. There is truly no need for such dramatics, especially if you only plan to be away for a limited period."

Clara nodded but persisted nonetheless. "I understand that, but I believe it's the prudent thing to do. I must be prepared for all eventualities, including my untimely demise. As you said, it's called the Wild West for a reason. There are bandits and kidnappers, and the society, from what I've read, appears to be somewhat lawless. Anything could happen to me out there, and I need to be prepared for it. Or, rather, you do. That's why I want you to draft my last will and testament, ensuring that my entire estate goes to my cousin. If something should happen to her, the proceeds should go to the Sisters of Mercy orphanage. Is that clear?"

Mr. Seymour nodded his head and looked at Clara with a questioning gaze. "Yes, my dear, I'll take care of that straight away. But you will be fine, Miss Clara. You've managed to navigate so much in your relatively short life; I have no doubt that you can handle this too. You will return before long, unharmed and as wise and level-headed as when you left."

Clara smiled at the lawyer and nodded. "Yes, I expect I shall. Thank you, Mr. Seymour. I may not see you for some time, so thank you and God bless."

"God bless you, my dear girl," Mr. Seymour said. He stood and leaned across the desk with his hand extended. Clara shook it with vigor and then turned to leave his office.

It was settled. She was going to Texas. She just hoped it would be a brief journey.

CHAPTER 3

The day of their departure came quickly, and Charity hadn't yet found a way to tell her stepfather about her plans. She knew he would be devilishly angry no matter how she broke the news that she was leaving. In the end, she decided to avoid discussing it with him altogether and waited instead until he was in his normal drunken state before making her escape. When she heard the telltale sounds of his snoring, she grabbed her carpetbag of clothes and personal items and snuck out of the tenement apartment.

The floorboards were made of old, creaky wood and, although Charity did her best to avoid making a noise, in her haste to reach the door, an offending floorboard cracked loudly and echoed off the thin walls. Her stepfather's snoring paused, and Charity's heart was beating so fast that she was sure it would burst through her chest, but then the snoring resumed. She was safe.

Clara met Charity outside her tenement building, frowning at the carpetbag in her hands. "Is that really all you're taking?" she asked as they made their way back to Clara's house, where they would spend the night.

"It's not as though I have very many possessions, Clara. A few dresses, my bible, and a hat were all I needed."

"What's the hat for?" Clara asked as they turned a street corner.

"To keep the sun off my skin, of course! The Texas climate isn't kind, you know. It's almost like the desert out there in places, I believe. Clayton might be a kind man, but that doesn't mean he'll want a woman with sunburnt skin and covered in freckles," Charity said.

Clara's house came into view as the women turned the next corner. She lived in a large brownstone in Brooklyn, a neighborhood populated by wealthy merchants. She had always loved her house, loved the stately way it stood on the street, and loved the soft stones that made up its exterior.

Clara couldn't believe this would be her the last night here, possibly for weeks. It would be the longest she had ever been away. Possibly forever. It was the only home she had ever known, and here she was abandoning it on a stupid whim. She knew the trip might be short, but not coming home each evening to her library and her quiet, respectful staff made her heart ache. She doubted she would find the same home comforts at the Ashmore Ranch in Texas.

Charity looked up at the house fondly. It reminded her of the home she had lost. If her father had recovered, she wouldn't be doing this. But here she was, about to go on the adventure of a lifetime.

Clara and Charity walked up to their respective rooms. Charity to the guest room next to Clara's master bedroom, where they caught a few hours of sleep before leaving for their train. Clara couldn't sleep. She thought of every single problem that might occur over the next few weeks. She tossed and turned all night, worried that their train might derail, that they might be robbed in their sleep, that the food served on the train would cause a stomach ailment that would kill them. Worries and anxieties swirled in Clara's head until finally, the sun began to rise, and beams of red light snuck in through her window, and she knew it was time to leave. Charity on the other hand slept like a baby. She thought it was due to the fact she didn't have to worry about James stumbling drunkenly into her bedroom.

Clara exchanged a tearful goodbye with her maid, Alice, as she stood at the doorway to the house an hour later. "Look after yourself, yes?" She told Alice. "You are in charge of the house. Look after it for me. And write to me if you need anything, anything at all. If it's an emergency, see Mr. Seymour. He can help you with anything I can't."

Alice held back a sob as she embraced Clara. Charity looked on sadly, realizing for the first time just how much her cousin was giving up to accompany her. While Charity had been desperate to escape New York City, Clara had no reason to leave. She loved the city, her house, and her job, and the quiet life she had made for herself. Charity vowed to make sure that she would make the journey to Texas worthwhile and that her engagement to Clayton would be short. Clara needed to be back in New York as soon as possible.

After more hugging and chatting, Clara stepped

away from Alice and straightened her fichu. "Right, well, we'll be off," she said, turning to Charity. They linked arms and, after Alice opened the door for them, walked out into the morning, heading to Grand Central Depot.

The train was just pulling out of the depot as the sun rose fully in the sky. Charity rarely had time to just sit and watch a sunrise. She had never before experienced the full beauty of dawn. It was breathtaking, and made her wonder if sunrises were the same the world over, and whether she would see the same thing when she looked out her window in the early dawn hours at River Creek, Texas.

The compartment she and Clara shared was spacious, being first class. The price had been exorbitant, but since it was their first time traveling aboard a train, Clara had thought the comfort was worth the expense. The inheritance from her parents meant she was more than able to afford it. When she paid for the tickets, she couldn't help but think that they had cost more than two months' wages. But her job had never been about the money. Most of what she had earned there went to the orphanage anyway. It was about waking up with a sense of purpose, having people to talk to and filling the long hours. She had been told that a husband and family would fill those hours just as well without the need to have her finger stuck with a needle all day. But she knew all of that would come later. Probably. Having money, she worried that men who showed interest were just after her wealth. It had resulted in her rejecting most male advances before they had even taken root.

Their trunks, including the one that Clara had insisted Charity use, were stacked on a small wooden shelf above their heads. To one side of the compartment were bunk beds made up with soft cotton sheets. To the other side was a small table and two benches, and this is where Clara was sitting, leaning her elbow against the window and watching as the morning light changed the color of the leaves on the trees as they passed.

"This was a terrible idea, a terrible idea, oh dear, oh dear," Clara was muttering under her breath, curled up on one of the beds with her arms around her knees.

Charity was so lost in thought that at first she didn't notice. When she did, she rushed to Clara's side. "Clara! Whatever is the matter?"

"I shouldn't have done this!" she cried, tears

streaking down her face. "This was a terrible idea! What if we're robbed or assaulted? We're two young ladies traveling on our own! Anything could happen to us!"

Charity wrapped her arms around her cousin and rocked her back and forth the way her mother used to when she had a nightmare as a child. Clara might be the older of the two of them, but parts of her mind were just as skittish as a little girl's, and it was to those that Charity was now catering. Clara's tears slowed and her breathing became more steady as Charity continued the soothing rocking motion. Soon, Clara was asleep, her head resting on Charity's shoulder. Charity laid her cousin out on the bed, unlaced her boots and pulled a blanket over her. She made sure Clara was fully asleep before quietly leaving the compartment in search of something to eat.

Three hours later, Clara woke up to Charity sitting across from her, paging through her bible and chewing mindlessly on an apple.

"What time is it?" Clara muttered, her mouth sticky and slack from sleep.

"Just after ten o'clock. If you hurry, you can still catch the tail end of the breakfast dining service,"

Charity said, looking up from her book and bestowing an indulgent smile on her cousin.

Clara began to rise. Throwing the blanket off, she stood in front of Charity. She stretched her arms over her head and bent down to touch her toes, and then stood straight. "Well, I am actually a little hungry. I think I'll go see if they have some bread or something for me to nibble on."

The dining car was only a minute's walk from the compartment Clara shared with her cousin, and she could smell the intoxicating aroma of fresh bread and eggs soon after she closed the door. Her mouth started to water as she opened the door and gazed down at the booths filled with passengers sipping tea and coffee, buttering rolls and slicing into bacon and scrambled eggs. Clara spied an empty booth towards the back of the car and made her way there.

"May I help you, ma'am?" a waiter asked soon after she had seated herself.

"Yes! Am I in time for breakfast?" she asked. The man nodded and handed Clara a menu of thick, creamy paper card. She scanned the offerings and decided that eggs with bacon and bread would satisfy the appetite that was suddenly raging within her. She placed her order and sat, watching the people around her while she waited for her food to arrive.

When it came, the bacon was crisped, and the eggs were perfectly scrambled with lashings of butter and cream obvious in the mixture. It was the best breakfast Clara had ever had, and she couldn't decide if that was because travel made a body hungry, or whether the fare offered in the dining car truly was exceptional. Either way, Clara had to hold herself back from swiping her finger through the remaining bacon grease on her plate.

"Was it to your satisfaction, ma'am?" the waiter asked when he came back to clear Clara's plate.

"Oh yes, very much so!"

The waiter smiled in response, and as Clara made her way back to her compartment, she began to admit that perhaps this journey would not be so terrible after all.

CHAPTER 4

Clara's optimism did not last.

Whatever happiness and contentment she had felt after breakfast abandoned her with the first slide of the compartment door later that day. It was a rail car worker, checking to make sure the women had enough blankets and towels, but the sight of a stranger in her personal space sent Clara into a fit.

Charity had to usher the woman out so that she could help Clara to lie down, pressing a cool cloth to her forehead and whispering, "It's all right, Clara. Don't worry, we're perfectly safe," over and over until Clara finally drifted off into a fitful sleep.

Her jumpiness continued over the next few

days. Any time someone opened the door to their compartment, whether a crew member bringing fresh linen, a waiter with the dinner that Charity ordered to their room, or in one instance, a lost passenger mistakenly happening upon their room. Clara had looked so frightened that Charity was beginning to wonder how her cousin had ever spoken to anyone new in her life. How was she able to live alone? Was Clara so afraid of strangers, or was it just the train and her perceived uncertainty about what awaited them that worried her so?

Thankfully, Charity had the chance to discuss this aloud rather than in her head, when she met a priest in the passageway on her way to the dining car on their fourth day on board.

"Why hello! I don't believe we've been introduced," the priest greeted Charity when they bumped into each other outside the compartment. "I'm Father Janice."

"Pleased to meet you, Father. I'm Charity Bryant. Would you perhaps care to join me for something to eat?"

After three days of eating in the compartment with Clara bemoaning the constant shaking of the train and how difficult eating was under the circumstances, Charity was more than ready for a different dinner companion. One who perhaps was willing to discuss anything other than the certain danger that awaited two women in Texas.

"I would love that, my dear child! Let us get ourselves to the dining car and see what special comestibles they have on offer this evening."

And so Charity spent a delightful two hours with Father Janice, talking about what had brought him on a train journey to Texas, how long he had been preaching, and what to do about Clara.

"Well, it sounds to me like you need to be honest with her, my child. If you like, I could accompany you back to your compartment and take tea with you and Clara. Perhaps I could put her mind at ease slightly, and then you and she will be able to enjoy the remainder of your journey."

Charity looked up from forking the last of the sponge cake on her plate. "Oh, would you, Father? That would be such a help. Perhaps she needs someone older, more responsible, to speak to. I'm younger than her, and I don't think she wants to open up to me and be vulnerable when she is meant to be the stronger, older one."

Father Janice took a deep gulp of his tea, then

stood up and set his napkin on the table. "Well then, to Clara we must go!"

As Charity suspected, Father Janice was able to work wonders with Clara. She opened up to the man more than she would have ever done otherwise; she told the priest about her fear of leaving the life she knew, a stable and comfortable existence, for this adventure to a new place and strange people.

"I'm just so worried I've made a mistake, Father," Clara divulged, looking worriedly at Charity before continuing. "Charity is my best friend in the world, and I want to help her so badly because she deserves a good life full of people who love her. But I am so worried that I have led us into an undesirable situation that will cause us both even more grief and suffering."

Father Janice nodded, waiting for Clara to finish. When she fell silent, looking at him with his frowning mouth, he said, "Have faith, child. God is watching over you, and He never gives us more than we are able to endure. Trust that all will be well. Trust God, trust yourself, and trust your cousin."

Clara nodded. "Thank you so much, Father. I am suddenly quite tired. I believe a rest before the evening meal is in order. Perhaps Charity and I might join you in the dining car?"

"Excellent," Father Janice said, standing and taking Clara's hands between his. "God bless you, my child."

Clara lay down as soon as the door to the compartment closed and slept for two hours. She looked peaceful and serene and, sitting across from her and reading her bible, Charity hoped that the talk with Father Janice had set Clara at ease. She hoped too that perhaps when she awoke, she would finally be able to start enjoying their trip.

However, when Clara awoke, the first words out of her mouth were not the optimistic platitudes that Charity had been hoping for. Instead, they were anxious ramblings, though the fright fueling them was turned up tenfold so that when Clara spoke, it was with wide eyes, pupils dilated as though she was watching a horrific scene play out in her mind.

"Have faith! How can I possibly have faith when I have made the worst decision of my life?" Clara said as she got up from the bed and began to pace the small square of carpet between the bed and the table where Charity was now sitting, shrinking further and further into her chair in defeat. "We should have never come on this trip, Charity. We should have stayed at home in New York and packed you up and moved you into my home. It was so unlikely that your stepfather would find you. After all, he was drunk most of the time anyway. It would have taken him weeks to find you, by which point I would have had Mr. Seymour hand him a sum of money that ensured he never bothered you again. We could have lived happily in that house for years to come, but instead we're on this stupid train that rocks back and forth so much that I can't get a sip of soup without spilling, in a tiny compartment with hardly any room. And when we get to River Creek, we will be received by two strange men whom we have never met. One of whom you are supposed to marry! This is a disaster!"

Charity sat up and reached for Clara's hand, stopping her cousin's pacing. "Clara, you must not work yourself up so. Come, sit across from me and take some deep breaths and we can talk through everything."

Clara did as Charity instructed, taking a seat across from her at the small table. She sat up straight with her hands laced primly in front of her on the table. Looking across at Charity, she shrugged and said, "Well? What is there to talk through? We've made a terrible mistake, and that is that."

Charity leaned across the table and placed her hands atop Clara's. "But we haven't. We are on an adventure together. No matter what happens, we will stay together. I love you, Clara. No matter what happens, I will not abandon you. I know you felt you had to accompany me to make sure I was safe, but I think this move will be good for you, too. After all, it's during times of difficulty that we learn the most about ourselves. Since my mother died, I've learned that I'm much stronger than I ever thought possible. And I think you're going to discover some very important truths about yourself once we reach River Creek."

Clara balked, "I doubt I'll be able to discover anything about myself because I'm sure those men will murder us the first chance they get."

"Is that what you really think? That we're in that much danger?"

"Of course! This is preposterous, us going to live with people we have never met before! It's preposterous, and not at all proper!"

And suddenly, Charity understood. She understood the root of all Clara's woes, and she knew exactly what to say to snap her cousin out of her spiraling pessimism.

"Clara," she whispered, grabbing her attention, because Charity never spoke quietly. She was loud by nature, vibrant and boisterous, so when her voice dropped, it signaled that she was about to say something truly memorable and important. "I know this is not easy. Your life has been turned upside down and when we get to Texas, it will no longer resemble what it was before. But one thing will be the same. Me. I will be there for you every step of the way, and I promise you will be able to return to New York just as soon as I am settled. This stay in Texas will not last forever for you. You will be back home in no time at all."

Clara nodded and tears began to form in her eyes. Charity kneeled beside her, hugging her close and letting Clara cry into her dress. "I'm so sorry," Clara whispered. "I've been spoiling this for you, haven't I?"

Charity nodded, figuring there was no use lying. "Yes. I was so looking forward to this trip, and the last few days have been miserable, trying to keep you happy and feeling like you won't be happy unless I'm miserable. I don't want to be miserable, Clara. I've spent months being sad about Mother and now I really want to feel happy and excited. I'm starting a new life."

Clara nodded again and leaned back, extricating herself from Charity's embrace. "Well then, happy and excited is what we shall be. I am going to freshen up and then we can join Father Janice for supper."

Charity watched her cousin shut the door to the bathroom and heard the splashing of water from the pitcher. She hoped that as Clara washed away her tears, she was washing her fears away, too.

CHAPTER 5

*R*iver Creek stop was growing near. Father Janice had disembarked from the train the previous day, and since then Clara and Charity had spent a companionable time reading to each other, having long, languid meals in the dining car, and telling each other stories. Clara was just finishing a tale about the woman she deemed the best-dressed woman in New York when the conductor's voice rang out through the train.

"RIVER CREEK! NEXT STOP RIVER CREEK!"

. . .

Both girls ran to the window, and there just half a mile ahead was the train station. It was a warm, sunny day, and the clear blue sky allowed Charity to just make out the figures of a few women, men and children waiting on the platform. She wondered which of them could be Clayton and whether he would look as she had pictured him in her mind.

Minutes later, the girls had repacked their trunks and were waiting in the passageway near the door. They were the first off the train when it stopped, with Clara helping Charity down the steep steps.

"Clara May? Charity Bryant?" a man asked from behind them. Both girls turned and were met with the shy, smiling face of a golden-haired man with soft brown eyes and an unruly brown beard.

"Yes, that's us!" Charity answered, eyeing the man appreciatively. If he was Clayton, he was even more handsome than she had imagined. He was tall, with a broad chest, his muscles visible even under the leather vest and white cotton shirt. He took off his hat and gave them each a little bow, his cheeks flushing as he straightened himself.

Charity liked him immediately. She walked forward and stuck her hand out the way she had seen men do, and after a moment, Clayton took it in his. His palms were rough, no doubt from the manual labor he performed, and his skin was tanned from so much time spent in the sun. After they shook hands, Clara greeted him likewise and then the three stood silently looking at each other.

Clayton was the first to break the silence. "Welcome! Why don't we walk to my horse and cart? It's just to the rear of the station, and the ride to the ranch should only take ten minutes. I'm sure you ladies are tired after your journey."

Charity and Clara followed Clayton through the small waiting room and out into the sunshine. He walked ahead to the horse and cart, untying the filly from the hitching post.

. . .

"He's so handsome, isn't he? Just beautiful, like something out of a Greek myth!" Charity whispered to Clara as they followed Clayton. Clara giggled but agreed.

"He seems very nice," she whispered as they stood beside the horse.

Clayton turned to them. "So, if we put your trunks in the cart, I think both of you can fit on the cart with me at the helm, so to say."

Clara looked apprehensively at the large horse which was even more imposing up close, but she tried to console herself in the knowledge that Clayton must be a seasoned horseman, and surely the horse wouldn't get out of control with him at the reins.

Clayton helped the girls onto the cart before hoisting himself onto the seat up front, and they were off. He kept the horse at a steady clip, slower than her normal pace, he told them. "I'm sure it's a bit unnerving your first time. I've been with horses for as long as I can remember, but I know some folks find horses, even ones as sweet as Maisy here, a bit intimidating."

"That's so kind of you, thank you," Charity said from behind him.

Clara clung tightly to her bench but forced herself to look around, admiring the scenery they passed on their way to the ranch. The town was small but seemed to have all a person could need: a lawyer, a sheriff, an undertaker, a saloon, and even the small market from which merchants were selling fresh produce and large sacks of what looked to be flour. She even spotted a small tailor shop and made a note to inquire if they might need a seamstress. If her stay was extended, Clara doubted she would be content languishing idly about. She would need to keep herself occupied.

. . .

Clara leaned in and whispered in Charity's ear, pointing as they passed the bank, "Look! No one is robbing the bank! This must be a good town." Charity looked back and gave her cousin an odd look, shook her head and turned to face the front.

They reached the ranch within ten minutes, and Clayton helped each lady off the cart before offloading their trunks.

"Now I ought to warn you before we go inside," he said as he took Maisy to the stables and gave her a carrot. "My brother, Edrick, isn't real happy at the idea of having two women in the house. We had a bit of an argument earlier about it and he stormed off in a huff, which is why he isn't here with me to welcome you. He's gotten so used to it being just the two of us that it'll be an adjustment, but don't pay him no mind. He'll settle down with time, and he should too, with ladies as lovely as you."

. . .

CLARA LOOKED over to catch Charity blushing and batting her eyelashes at Clayton, and laughed to herself. The girl was already flirting and they'd only been in River Creek for twenty minutes.

Charity and Clara followed Clayton as he carried their trunks to the house. "Did you see the way he was looking at me?" Charity whispered to her cousin as they walked. "I think he's fond of me already!"

CLARA TURNED to her Charity and smiled, "Yes, I'm sure he is."

AS THEY WALKED, Clayton pointed out anything of interest on the ranch. "Over there is the herd, and just beyond is the barn we hold them in when we must and when we can get them in. Over here is the house Edrick and I share. It's real warm inside and comfortable, too, so let's get you ladies settled."

CLAYTON LED the way up the stairs to the porch and set the trunks down on the hard wood floor before opening the door and allowing the women to enter ahead of him. The first thing that struck Charity about the house was the complete lack of a feminine touch. There were no blankets or rugs to add color and coziness, no flowers on the table or books by the fire. Nothing to indicate that the men did anything other than use the house for shelter.

CLAYTON SHOWED the girls to the bedroom they would be sharing, and Clara was struck by its simplicity. The threadbare blanket covering the bed was a muted grey, and the only adornments, although practical, were a pair of candlesticks on the bedside table. The room lacked personality and Clara longed for the comfort of her room back in New York, filled with all her things and brightened with pinks and reds draped all about that never failed to make her smile when she opened the door.

"THIS ROOM IS ABSOLUTELY WONDERFUL," Charity told Clayton as he entered behind them and deposited their trunks at the foot of the bed. "Thank you so much for your hospitality."

. . .

The blush on Clayton's face was immediate, climbing from his neck up to his cheeks until both were a bright, rose pink. "Oh, uh, thank you kindly, Charity. I'm glad it's to your liking. Please, make yourselves at home. I have things to attend to in the fields, so I need to get back to work. The ranch never sleeps, so to speak."

Clara stood up from where she had been fussing with her trunk. "That's absolutely fine. Why don't we prepare you and Edrick some supper while you're working? It's the least we can do after you welcomed us into your home so graciously."

Again, Clayton blushed. He stammered out a "thank you kindly" before leaving the room and walking briskly to the front door. The door slammed behind him, signaling his departure. Once again, Clara and Charity were alone together.

. . .

"Well, shall we get started on that supper? Perhaps we can find some flowers somewhere to put on the table to spruce things up a little," Charity said as they made their way back into the kitchen.

"Yes, let's. This house is in desperate need of some decoration."

CHAPTER 6

Charity and Clara managed to find vegetables and meat cuts in the area that served as a pantry, and they soon set about preparing a stew. While they chopped and stirred, Charity gushed about Clayton, saying how she couldn't believe how handsome and kind and gracious he was. "He's so much better than I ever could have imagined. He's just perfect, isn't he, Clara?"

Clara was reluctant to jump to conclusions about a man they had only met hours before, but she nodded, knowing that Charity wouldn't appreciate her suggestion to reserve judgment on Clayton until she knew him better.

The stew was bubbling away, and Charity had

just returned with a posy of colorful wild flowers when Clara heard voices outside. "Aren't these just the prettiest pink you've ever…" Charity was saying when Clara shushed her, intent on hearing what the men had to say. There was Clayton's voice and another's, Edrick's, Clara guessed. His voice was deeper than Clayton's. He sounded older, and his words were spoken in anger.

"I know we're meant to be compassionate since his wife died, but honestly, Clayton, he's just not working well. He's too distracted, and if we have to give him extra wages for one more month because of that crippled son of his, we're going to be in trouble. Others will start expecting it. How can we say no then?"

Clara was shocked by what she heard. She wasn't aware of the circumstances, of course. But how could a man be so cruel, especially to one of his employees? If that was Edrick's voice she heard, she wasn't so sure she could be sympathetic to the man, even if he was a widower.

Clara looked to her side and found Charity in a similar state of shock, but they had no time to discuss what they had heard before the door to the house was thrown open and a tall, muscular redhead walked in. Edrick was indeed older than

Clayton by about ten years, and his body was muscular and clearly toned by honest, hard labor. He cut an imposing figure as he stood in the doorway looking at Clara and Charity.

Edrick looked questioningly at Clayton who stood up straight and with false brightness, as though he knew his next words would not please his brother, "Edrick! Meet Charity Bryant and Clara May, the lovely young women I was telling you were coming to stay with us. They arrived in River Creek only this afternoon and offered to prepare us supper! Isn't that nice of them?"

Edrick frowned and didn't respond right away, but after a subtle nudge in the side from, Clayton's elbow, he said, "Yes. I remember. You're still going through with this then?" He didn't wait for a response before heading for what Clara assumed was his room, off to the right of the kitchen. Clara couldn't help but feel her initial assessment of him had been correct: he was rude. He didn't even say hello, did he?

But despite her feelings toward him, Clara made an effort as they sat down to supper, to get to know the man who clearly didn't want them there. As Charity and Clayton spoke about the ranch and flowers and cattle and seemingly every other subject under the sun, Clara asked Edrick how his day had been.

"Fine," was his response. When she asked him whether the weather would grow any colder in the coming weeks, he said, "Perhaps."

Trying to engage him in a conversation about books, sewing, food, cattle and the town itself was met with similar responses. Finally, Clara gave up and ate the rest of her dinner in silence, listening as Charity and Clayton got to know each other from their seats around the table. Clara offered to do the washing up after the meal and took solace in the fact that even if Edrick hadn't spoken more than a few words to her, he had at least enjoyed the meal. His plate was licked clean of any juice left from the stew, and she had seen him pat his belly appreciatively as he adjourned to his room after the meal. At least he enjoyed her cooking, Clara mused. And she need not wash up since it was then that their chaperone presented herself in the form of the elderly grandmother of a ranch worker, whose extended family lived on the ranch. She wasn't going to be staying the night, but at least it was another female to talk to while her cousin stared dreamy-eyed at the man she was going to wed. She rather thought that this would be a token visit and the woman wouldn't be seen again, but at least Clayton had gone to the trouble. Watching her cousin edge her chair closer to the handsome cowboy, Clara knew that she was already smitten.

Over the next few days, Charity got to know Clayton. She found the man to be both kind and shy. The more they got to know one another, the more he opened up. Although Clayton was busy most mornings tending to the cattle, he took a break around eleven each day. During that time, he and Charity walked around the fields and, occasionally, to town. At first, Clara trailed behind them, making sure things stayed proper, but once she realized that Clayton was responsible and wouldn't take advantage of Charity, she left them to their own devices.

"He's so kind, Clara. And so introspective. We were discussing some of the biblical psalms I've been reading and his interpretation of them is so intelligent. So much goes on in that mind of his, I tell you," Charity divulged as they stood before the stove one evening stirring the stew for supper.

"Well, I'm glad to hear it. He does seem a good, kind man. Perfect for you, really. I shouldn't have doubted his character. He's just like you said he was in his letters."

Charity looked up from chopping meat for the stew and smiled. "He is, isn't he?

Though I wonder how Edrick is so different to him. He seems so stoic, does he not? Perhaps he is the strong, silent type, but I assumed he would make more of an effort to get to know the two of us, didn't you?"

Charity looked at her cousin, who simply shrugged. Clara was not one to mince words, so Charity was surprised and a little worried at the silence. "Oh no, what is it?" she asked, worried that Clara was keeping something from her.

"It isn't his lack of conversation that has me troubled. He's bitter, Charity. I've overheard him complaining time and time again about the finances of the ranch, saying that certain workers are a drain on funds. You heard it yourself on the first day we were here. He even complained about lending money to a ranch hand whose wife has died and whose son is crippled!"

Charity nodded, remembering the conversation, but before she could answer, Clara continued, "I'm sure that life out here is hard, especially with the size of the herd and land that Edrick and Clayton have to manage, but he seems capable only of negative comments about his lot and his workers. I worry that he will have an undue influence on the household, even when you marry Clayton. You know how traits go in families. What happens if, as Clayton grows older, his character changes to become more like his brother? It's just an observation, nothing more."

Charity thought for a moment. "We have to remember that the man has seen his wife die. That has to change a person. Make them question everything. Now with my arrival, there is going to be more change on the horizon. I think it's just a barrier, something he puts up in an attempt to shield himself from pain."

Clara nodded. Her cousin never stopped amazing her. Sometimes her insights were so thoughtful. She vowed that she would be more understanding.

CHAPTER 7

After her talk with Charity, Clara tried to make more of an effort with Edrick, but to no avail. He remained cold and silent with her. Clara was thinking more seriously about inquiring about a seamstress position in town simply to get out of the house each day until she returned to New York. But she was wary of upsetting the men, who seemed to depend on her and Charity for housekeeping and food. She decided it would be foolish to accept a job for the few weeks she was likely to be in River Creek. So it was that she began to take daily walks around the fields in the afternoon instead.

The walks helped to clear her mind. The landscape was so different from the bustling city streets of New York. It was peaceful and relaxing. If someone wanted to, they could go for days or even weeks without seeing another living soul. The silence was the amazing thing. Clara found she liked the silence interrupted by the occasional lowing of the cattle.

One day Clara's walk took her toward the houses occupied by the ranch hands. She had passed by them before, but never this close.

"Miss! Miss!" she heard a small voice calling to her. Clara looked over and saw a young boy of about six or seven sitting on the ground outside a small house.

"Why, hello there. What are you doing on the ground?" Clara asked, walking closer to the boy. As she approached him, she saw that he was sitting oddly. One leg was bent beneath him, while the other was stretched out. The knee was awkwardly bent, and his calf looked almost twisted around. She realized this must be the boy that Edrick had mentioned as the crippled one whose father had asked Edrick for a loan.

"I'm drawing. Would you like to help?" the boy asked, pointing at the sketch he had drawn in the dirt with the stick in his hand. Clara crouched down in front of him and for the next few minutes they worked silently together, drawing flowers and grass outside of a house, with a small cow just to its side.

"You're very good at this. Have you done it before, miss?" the boy asked. Clara shook her head.

"No, I can't say I have. Do you do this often?" she asked him. The boy looked up at her and beamed, showing off the gap where his two front milk teeth had once been.

"All the time! My papa reads to me when he's not working, but while he's with the cattle, I sit here and draw all day long. I love to draw."

Clara smiled at him but jumped when she heard, "Jacob! What are you doing?" from behind her.

She turned and came face to face with the ranch hand who, upon seeing Clara, halted. "Miss, what can I do for you on this fine day?" he asked, removing his hat.

"Oh, I was just passing by and was invited to draw by your boy. He's an excellent artist."

The man nodded and walked toward Jacob, helping the boy to stand. "That he is, miss. Am I correct in thinking you're one of the ladies living in the ranch house with the bosses?"

Clara nodded. "Yes, I'm Clara May," she introduced herself, holding out her hand. "My cousin is planning to marry Clayton. I'll return to my home in the city after the wedding."

The man shook her hand and introduced himself, "I'm Billy, and this here is Jacob," he said, looking down at his son.

"It's a pleasure to make your acquaintance," Clara said.

Billy and Jacob invited Clara in for a cup of coffee, and she spent a pleasant hour in their small but comfortable home. She learned that Billy was the same age as Clayton and had worked for the brothers since he was a young boy. "My papa worked for their daddy, it was only natural I continued," Billy said before taking a sip of coffee from a small, dented tin cup.

"So this ranch has been around for some time?" Clara asked. Clayton hadn't told them its history. Since she supposed it was now her temporary home, she was curious as to how long the ranch had been around.

"A long time in the scheme of things out here, and the Ashmores have always been good employers. Good men, too," Billy said.

"Clayton is the best man, other than my papa. He visits me every week and draws with me, and sometimes he reads to me, too. We just started The Gospel of Matthew this week," Jacob said from where he was sitting across from Clara, swinging his legs idly underneath the chair.

"And does Edrick visit you as well?" Clara couldn't help asking. If he was complaining so often about Billy and Jacob, he must see them quite frequently.

"Edrick! He's such a mean man. I don't like him. He never comes here and thank goodness for that!" Jacob said, yelling the last bit for emphasis.

Billy looked at Clara with embarrassment and then turned to Jacob. "Now, boy, you know we don't say unkind things about people, especially not those who have helped us so much. Edrick has been as good to us as Clayton. He's just quieter. Keeps himself to himself. And ain't nothing wrong with that. A quiet man can still be a good one," Billy admonished. Jacob nodded mutely and returned to swinging his legs.

Clara couldn't help but wonder why Edrick was so concerned with Billy and his boy if he never saw them. She knew enough about finances to know the ranch was doing very well indeed, and surely they had more than enough money to spare to help Billy and Jacob through their difficult time.

Billy was obviously a loyal worker, and she couldn't imagine how hard it must be for him to toil away at the ranch during the day while making the time to travel to far away towns to have Jacob seen by the best doctors.

Billy told Clara on her way out that Jacob had to see a doctor a few towns over regularly to check on his knee; if it grew worse, they would have to amputate. Clara's heart broke at the thought of such an energetic young boy losing a limb. She resolved to do whatever she could to help Billy and Jacob. She made her way back to the ranch, wondering what had caused Edrick to be so apathetic to the struggles of Billy Morris and his child. They deserved nothing but kindness, and she wondered why a man as wealthy and privileged as Edrick couldn't give as much.

CHAPTER 8

"Where have you been all afternoon?" Charity asked, seated at the table paging through her bible. Clara had just walked in, her cheeks flushed from the cold, and a small empty basket in her hands.

"I've been out visiting Billy and Jacob, the rancher and his son who live in one of the small houses on the property."

Charity looked up from her bible, "Oh? You seem to be seeing a lot of them lately."

"Well, yes. It's clear Jacob isn't being properly fed, and he's all alone in that house all day while his father toils on the ranch. It isn't right, and it's not as though I have much else to fill my time. I'd rather stop by their home and bring them what I can to make sure Jacob is well-fed and comfortable, than attempt to get Edrick to talk to me."

"I'm so sorry Edrick isn't as welcoming as he might be. I understand it makes it difficult. I tried to speak to Clayton about it, but he said that since Edrick's wife's death, he's been so closed off and cold. Apparently, he used to be quite talkative and open, but losing his wife so suddenly seems to have changed him."

Clara nodded. She had assumed as much, but despite feeling for the man and his tragedy, she still could not fathom why he couldn't make a small effort. After all, he knew that she wasn't going to be here forever. The only time he seemed capable of speaking was during meals. It was as though manners seemed to be forgotten out here.

And that night was no different. While Clara dished out the meal, Edrick tucked in and moans of pleasure escaped him as he spooned the hot beef into his mouth. "This is right good, Clara," he complimented.

"Oh! Thank you, Edrick. I'm pleased you like it," she said, shocked that he had even mentioned her by name.

Edrick paused and looked up at her, meeting her eyes for the first time. "It's just like my mama used to make," then, he turned to Clayton. "Isn't it, brother?"

Clayton nodded, and Clara didn't miss the smile quirking the corners of his mouth as he and Charity shared a secret look.

After such a successful meal, Clara thought it might be time to raise the issue of Billy and Jacob with Edrick. He seemed in a good mood as he sat by the fire, smoking his pipe and staring into the flames. While Clayton and Charity cleaned up after the meal, Clara took the chair opposite Edrick. He looked up as she spoke.

"Edrick, I was hoping to speak to you about one of the ranch hands, Billy Morris. He and his son Jacob, as you know, are all alone in one of the worker's cabins without a woman to care for or cook for them. The last few times I've visited them, I've noticed that Jacob is sorely underfed. He's just skin and bones, and the lack of nourishment can't be good for his condition. I wonder if we might be able to do anything for them, to give them some rations perhaps, to ensure they're both well cared for. When I managed a household, I found that the better my workers were taken care of, the more industrious they were."

Edrick looked over at Clara and puffed on his

pipe for a few moments, pondering her words. Then he turned to face her and for the second time that night, he looked deep into her eyes. Clara noticed that his were a deep emerald green that offset the ginger in his beard and hair. His skin was dark from so much time outside, but freckles were scattered across his cheeks, nose and forehead, lending him a youthful look that belied his strength and maturity.

"Now you listen here. Not that it is any of your business whatsoever, but I'll share a few things with you. I don't expect you to understand. But share them I will since you have seen fit to stick your nose into the running of this place. Billy Morris is nothing but a lazy good-for-nothing. And if it weren't for that boy, I would have kicked them out on their behinds long ago. They're nothing but a drain on the Ashmore Ranch, and that boy is a liability. He'll never be able to work with that knee of his. Keeping him and his pa on the land only serves to waste more money than ever before. If Clayton would let me," Edrick said, looking over to his brother and Charity, who had paused their chores and were watching his outburst in fascinated horror, "I'd have booted those Morris men out long ago. It's people like that who make it so hard for me to run my business. I'm not a philanthropist and they're not a charity case. I'm a ranch owner and I care about my cattle, and if a man can't take care of them cows, he has no place on this land."

And with that, Edrick rose from his chair so abruptly that the chair toppled backward behind him. He stomped out into the night, muttering about needing to check on the cattle. Clara was speechless with shock, watching him go, and jumped as the door slammed behind him.

"I don't understand," she whispered. "How could anyone be so mean?"

She heard Clayton's soft footsteps behind her. He righted Edrick's chair and sat in it, with Charity hovering just behind him.

"I'm so sorry, Clara. I know that sounded mighty cruel, but you have to understand where he's coming from. Our mama, God rest her soul, was always worried about money. When disease blew through the area and killed half our herd, we nearly went bankrupt, and all her fears were realized. Edrick was a young man at that point, and I think he absorbed all our mama's worries. Even now, when we're so successful and doing so well, he can't get it out of that head of his that one day we'll be back to pinching pennies. I'm not excusing his actions, merely explaining why he is the way he is."

Clara looked up at Charity, who shrugged with a look on her face that said 'well, what are you gonna do?'

"I understand his fears," Clara said. "But why is he so harsh with Billy? From all I've seen, the man is a good worker. He doesn't use Jacob as an excuse to beg off his duties. If anything, he works harder because of Jacob."

Clayton nodded, then cleared his throat, "It's Billy's wife. She died after a tragic accident in their cabin when she was pregnant, the same way that Edrick lost his wife. I think the tragedy with Mrs. Morris reminded Edrick of his own. Olivia begged and begged Edrick for a maid to help her around the house, but he refused, saying it was a waste of money and that he could do more than a maid ever could. But it was our busy season at the ranch, with lots of markets and Edrick was in town every other day. One day while we were all away it just happened. Poor Olivia; we found her dead when we returned, just lying at the bottom of the porch stairs. Edrick blames himself and, by extension, Billy for letting his wife come to the same fate."

"Oh dear, how awful!" Clara said, tears in her eyes. Knowing this put Edrick in a new light. He wasn't just a cruel, harsh man who wouldn't open up or let anyone in. He was a man grieving for his wife and angry with himself for the part he believed he had played in her death.

"Indeed. But you should know, Clara, that while he might still be silent and gruff around you, your presence, and yours, Charity," Clayton said, turning around to look at Charity, "has improved his mood so much. I even caught him smiling the other day when he thought I wasn't looking!"

"A smile on Edrick's face? That would be a sight to see," Clara laughed.

Clayton and Charity couldn't help but to join in.

CHAPTER 9

A few mornings later, Clara woke to find Charity sitting on the edge of her bed, already dressed, with her hair pinned back and her face freshly washed.

"What is it?" Clara asked, her voice still thick with sleep. A glance at the curtains opposite her bed told her it was early morning, the sun just cresting over the fields.

"I have something to tell you," Charity said excitedly, bouncing up and down on the straw mattress. Clara sat up and rubbed her eyes. It was far too early for Charity to be so energetic.

"What is it, Charity?" she asked, a note of annoyance in her voice.

"Clayton and I are to be wed! Tuesday next, we

will all go down to the chapel." Charity clapped her hands excitedly and jumped up from the bed to pace back and forth in front of the window. "Isn't it wonderful? He's such a good man, Clara, even better than I imagined. He's so kind and gentle and warm, and I feel so comfortable around him like he loves me just as I am. Because I do know he loves me. He…he told me so last week. And again last night when he proposed. It was nice of him to do it again, in person, as opposed to just by the letter."

Clara couldn't help but smile at seeing her cousin so happy. "He certainly will make you an excellent husband, Charity. I couldn't be happier for you. You deserve someone as kind as Clayton."

Clara had seen Clayton and Charity steal a kiss out by the pond the night before. They were clearly smitten with each other, and Clara had thought that it was only a matter of time before Clayton pressed the matter of their wedding. She'd rushed home after catching them and jumped in bed, pretending to be asleep when Charity came in a few minutes later.

Although Clara knew it wasn't proper for Charity and Clayton to be kissing and embracing before the wedding, she couldn't begrudge her cousin the happiness that came from a warm embrace from the man she loved. Clara longed for the very same. She had been taking care of herself since she was much younger after losing her parents in a fire. She found herself wishing more and more that for once, someone would look after her. She was twenty-six and unmarried, and no man had ever shown the least measure of interest in her. How she wished that would change.

Charity stopped pacing and sat across from Clara on her bed, reading her mind, "I've been praying that a man shows you the same kindness and love that Clayton has shown me. Perhaps even Edrick! After all, he and Clayton are brothers, cut from the same cloth. Edrick must be capable of the same depth of emotion. I know you've had your problems with him, but perhaps in time you'll grow on each other. Or maybe you'll meet a man back home. I just so wish to see you settled and happy like I am, Clara."

Clara snorted and rose from her bed to begin dressing. She held the same hope in her heart, but she doubted it would ever come to fruition. She doubted there was a man for her in the world. "I'm just happy to see you happy, Charity. That's what we came to River Creek for in the first place. You deserve a good life with a good man by your side."

Charity rose from her bed and wrapped her arms around Clara. "So do you, Clara. So do you," she whispered in her ear before stepping back and turning Clara around to help her with her hair. Clara relaxed as Charity began plaiting, and for a few moments she felt the first sense of real peace she had experienced since arriving in River Creek. Charity was happy. Nothing else mattered.

Clara couldn't sleep that night and began her day with early morning walks, traversing the fields when everyone on the ranch was still fast asleep. The quiet, misty spring mornings helped her think more about what she wanted out of life. Charity would soon be married and settling in with Clayton in the main ranch house, and Clara didn't want to impose on their time as newlyweds. They needed to acclimatize to living together as man and wife, and she didn't want her presence interfering.

This meant that she needed to return home to New York. She knew this was the right course of action and the best thing to do, but she just couldn't decide what kind of life she wanted for herself when she set foot back in her home city. She knew that she could easily fall back into the comfortable routine of working at the tailor's on Tuesdays and Thursdays and helping at the local orphanage on Fridays. Clara knew that doing so wouldn't satisfy her now that she'd had a taste, albeit a small one, of the adventure beyond her comfort zone.

She could only continue challenging herself, and that meant returning to New York to try out new ventures. But what could those be? Her world before leaving for River Creek had been so small; now, the possibilities seemed endless, and she couldn't choose.

Clara had been walking for what felt like miles, lost in this train of thought when she heard the crack of a small twig behind her, the sound amplified in the quiet of the early morning. Whipping around, she was surprised to see Edrick behind her.

His hair was a brighter red in the morning sunlight, the sun's rays picking up shades of deep auburn and gold in his long strands. He hadn't yet shaved, and a stubble of dark brown covered his strong, muscular jaw, accentuating his bone structure. His shirt was unbuttoned slightly, baring a small triangle of skin and chest hair to the world, and Clara couldn't help an intake of breath at the sight of him. He was so handsome, more handsome than she had ever realized before this moment.

"Good m-morning," Clara stuttered, suddenly incapable of comprehensible speech. She had never had trouble speaking to him before, but then again, he had never looked quite like this.

Edrick didn't respond; he simply stared at her, his eyes both fierce and inquiring and, if she wasn't mistaken, slightly guilty. Clara realized he might be feeling bad about their verbal altercation and that he may have followed her to apologize. But a man such as Edrick didn't strike her as one who would make the first move to repent for his actions, so Clara took the lead. "I-I'm sorry for what I said. Obviously, the ranch is your business, your home, and I should not be interfering. What I said was said out of goodwill, but I realize now how insulting it must have sounded. I hope you can accept my most sincere apology, Edrick. I truly meant no insult to the way you run the ranch."

Edrick looked away and then nodded and grunted, following the sound up with a muttered, "Accepted." He turned around, as though to head back to the ranch house, but then suddenly turned back and took a step toward Clara. "Be careful if you're walking near the river. It's very slippery and you can easily hurt yourself on the rocks." He said these words with a look of fierce intensity in his eyes that Clara couldn't quite read.

Clara nodded, amazed that he cared enough about her to give her such a warning, but grateful nonetheless. She still knew so little about the ranch and its surroundings, not least of all the dangers that lurked thereabouts.

Clara continued her walk, but instead of contemplating her future, her thoughts were now firmly rooted in the present and the recent interaction. Edrick was such a complicated man. She thought of the harsh set of his jaw that only seemed to loosen when he was eating. She thought of him losing his wife and blaming himself. She thought of how broken and angry he must be inside, of how difficult it must be to wake up every day blaming oneself for the loss of a beloved. Perhaps that guilt and anger had eaten away at him, making it harder for him to see the good in life, and the good in others, like Billy and Jacob.

Edrick was a difficult man to figure out, but as Clara walked, she suddenly realized that perhaps he wasn't the harsh man she thought he was. Maybe he was simply wounded and unable to heal.

Clara rounded the fields of cattle, taking a moment to admire their strong bodies as they grazed. A few looked at her curiously, but she knew from experience that they were sweet animals. They loved affection, and Clara laughed that she had ever been afraid of them. Her life in River Creek had turned out so different to what she imagined.

Her walk took her to the Morrises, the small shack illuminated by the sunlight and the bright blue sky. The sun had fully risen, and she knew that Billy would soon be leaving to begin his workday. Perhaps she could spend a few hours with Jacob, playing and drawing with him while his father worked. Though she had loved the children she worked with at the orphanage, there was something so special about placing all her attention on one child, doing whatever she could to make sure he succeeded in life. It almost made up for her own lack of children.

CHAPTER 10

*E*drick tightened the girth of the saddle around his horse, Herbert, and set off on his daily ride around the ranch. Since Olivia's death, he'd not been able to sleep, tossing and turning all night and always waking just before dawn to feel the cold side of the bed beside him, a daily reminder that his love was gone forever, and that it was all his fault. The brisk horseback ride allowed the constant dialogue of his guilty conscience over his wife's death to quiet for an hour or two, and he took in great gulps of fresh air as he flicked the reins and he and Herbert began flying across the land.

. . .

Down through the fields, past the cattle and horse barn, the river, and down toward the ranch hand houses he went, barely noticing the scenery as he passed. All he was interested in was the feeling of the wind in his hair, the warmth of the sun on his back; those simple pleasures a man could appreciate during a horse ride.

But when he heard the soft giggle he recognized as that of Clara May, he suddenly crashed back down to earth, remembering who and where he was. Edrick reined the horse in lightly, signaling for Herbert to slow down. Drawing closer, Edrick saw Clara sitting outside Billy Morris' small house, kneeling on the porch with Billy's son Jacob at her side. They were using sticks to draw what looked like letters in the soft, packed red dirt.

"J. A. C. O. Nearly there! What comes after O, Jacob?" Clara asked in the lilting voice that never failed to set Edrick's heart alight.

"B!" Jacob screamed excitedly.

. . .

"Yes! Excellent work, Jacob! Now draw it for me," Clara said, handing him the stick.

Edrick watched as Jacob slowly and carefully drew a large letter 'b' in the sand, his brow furrowed, and his tongue stuck between his teeth in concentration. Edrick realized that Clara must be teaching the boy to spell, and all at once his heart warmed even more.

So this was why she was so concerned with the Morrises. He had wondered what she did all day while he and Clayton worked the fields, and now he knew. Clara May, an upper-class woman if there ever was one, spent her days kneeling in the dirt, playing with Jacob Morris and teaching him his letters. She was an even better woman than he thought, and Edrick couldn't help the grin that creased the corners of his mouth as he watched Clara and Jacob, admiring the gentle, reverent way in which she spoke and played with the boy.

As he rode off down the fields some time later,

over the fence and toward town, the image of Clara's eyes closing in laughter at Jacob's words, played over and over in his head, burning the beautiful woman's smile into his brain. An image he knew he would return to frequently.

Clara was nearly finished with dinner when Charity came in from her pre-dinner walk with Clayton.

"Oh, it's just so beautiful out tonight, isn't it?" Charity gushed as she and Clayton came inside. Her cheeks were glowing pink from the slight chill in the air and she was beaming from ear to ear as she removed her cloak and sat down on a kitchen chair to fix the boot lace which had become untied.

"Yes, it is, isn't it, my sweet," Clayton agreed, staring dopily down at Charity. Since announcing the date, Clayton and Charity had grown even more smitten, staring at one another with love and devotion. It made Clara happy and also incredibly jealous and not a little queasy. Although she tried to remind herself that, if the storybooks were to be believed, this was what young love was all about. She was glad, however, that she would not have to bear the saccharine sweetness of their love for much longer. New York would provide a welcome respite in that regard.

"IT DOES LOOK LOVELY OUT. Dinner is almost ready, so why don't you help me set the table, Charity? While Clayton cleans up and calls for Edrick."

CHARITY NODDED, stood and walked over to the small chest of drawers off to the side of the kitchen near the stove where the crockery and cutlery were kept. Clayton cast her a long, lingering look before going to his room to change.

CHARITY WAS JUST LAYING the final knife on the table when Edrick walked in, sweaty and with a scowl on his face that seemed to clear the moment he caught sight of Clara at the stove and caught a whiff of whatever was in the pot she was stirring.

"Hello, Edrick. Dinner is nearly ready," Charity said, hearing his telltale footfalls and turning to him. Edrick was staring at her openly, causing Charity to eye the man curiously. He seemed frozen in place, staring at the back of Clara's head with rapt attention.

"Edrick? Edrick, are you listening?" Charity snapped him out of his reverie. Edrick grunted in response and stalked off to his room, but she didn't miss the blush coloring his cheeks as he left.

"He's acting a bit strange today, isn't he?" Charity whispered to Clara as she helped her cousin carry the bowls of soup and the basket of freshly baked bread rolls over to the table.

"Whatever do you mean?" Clara asked, puzzled. From where she stood, the interaction between

Charity and Edrick sounded fairly normal; after all, Edrick rarely did more than grunt in response to questions or statements. That he had actually spoken a full sentence to her this morning had truly shocked her.

"He was blushing when he left! And he was staring at your hair! It was very odd," Charity commented, looking over at Clara.

Clara shrugged and sat down to wait for Clayton and Edrick. Far be it for her to try to decipher the motives of Edrick Ashmore. She had far more important things to think about, such as Charity's reaction when she told her she was leaving for New York after the wedding. She planned to break the news that night over dinner, and she hoped her cousin would bear the news well. She feared however that she would be hurt, or worse, try to convince her to stay, an act that would be ultimately futile. Clara's mind was set, and there was no changing it.

. . .

After playing with Jacob that morning, Clara had had time to contemplate her next move, and decided that going back to New York and setting up her own charity for boys like Jacob would be her project. It would get her out of the privileged circles in which she usually moved and allow her to do some good with her money. While she wouldn't be able to devote as much attention as she gave Jacob to every child, she hoped that by spending time with the boys, teaching them and giving them money for schooling, clothes and food, she could imbue their life with enough positivity and resources to ensure they achieved whatever their hearts desired, no matter their circumstances.

Expending all her energy on the charity would also mean she would not have time to miss River Creek, which she was starting to grow rather fond of. Still, she knew that leaving was the right decision. She could feel it in her bones, but she didn't know if her best friend would feel the same way. She and Charity were so close and she knew that her cousin depended on her for so many things. She only hoped that Clayton could provide

Charity with enough love and companionship and friendship that she would not feel bereft when Clara left.

MOMENTS LATER, they were seated at the table and all tucking into their stew when Clara decided that now was as good a time as any to break the news. Perhaps everyone would be too distracted by the food to argue with her. She had made an outstanding stew, if she did say so herself.

"I HAVE DECIDED to return to New York City next week, two days after the wedding. I believe my job here, as it were, is done."

The sounds of spoons scraping bowls and chewing stopped, and all eyes were on Clara. Clayton was the first to speak. "But, Clara! We love having you here. You've become a part of the ranch, an institution. You can't leave."

CHARITY WAS NEXT, putting down her spoon and turning to fully face Clara. "Don't be silly, you can't leave just yet. Just because I'm marrying Clayton, doesn't mean I don't need you anymore. And besides, Billy and Jacob will miss you so, and didn't you say you were going to get a job in town as a seamstress? You haven't even really explored River Creek yet. You can't leave!"

Clara was surprised to see that Edrick also looked distressed at the news. Though his words were not said in the same aggrieved tone as Clayton's or Charity's, they were no less powerful, "Stay. You should stay."

Charity and Clayton exchanged a surprised look, as though flabbergasted that Edrick had spoken. But they continued, with Clayton saying, "Clara, please reconsider. New York will always be there for you, but Charity is right. You've barely even seen River Creek. You've only been here a few weeks. Give it a bit more time, please. We need you here. I'd be ever so sad if you left so soon."

"Yes, Clayton is right. At least give it a few more weeks. There is nothing back in the city that won't wait." Charity agreed, her eyes full of desperation, her tone imploring Clara to reconsider.

Clara shook her head. "No. I came here to see to it that Charity traveled safely to River Creek and that her marriage to Clayton was suitable. Now that both have been seen to, it's time I head home. I'm a liability to you all, an impediment to your ability to get to know each other as a family unit."

"But you are family, Clara. Mine and Clayton's. And Edrick's too," Charity said, with tears in her eyes, turning to look at the men who nodded silently.

"You're kind, Charity, but I need to leave. Trust me when I say that it is for the best for all of us." Silence followed this statement, followed by more arguments that lasted well into the meal, ruining the calm atmosphere and dissuading Clara from eating any more of the stew she had spent so long slaving over.

. . .

When she would not speak anymore on the subject, tired of hearing the arguments against her leaving, Clara got up and sliced into the pie she had baked earlier that day. She hoped that the sweetness of the apples and crust would soothe the wounds that had clearly been created by the discussion. The four tucked hungrily into the dessert, avoiding conversation as they went back to eating. The atmosphere was noticeably tense. Clara excused herself from the table as soon as she had finished her slice and was in bed by the time Charity had helped Grandmama wash and dry the pots and pans.

Clara was exhausted and nearly asleep when she heard her cousin's soft footsteps tiptoeing toward her.

"Clara? Clara, are you awake?" Charity whispered from somewhere near Clara's head.

Clara groaned and sat up, angry at the interruption. "Yes, I'm awake. What is it?" she snapped, not looking forward to more tearful begging from her cousin.

Charity ignored the snap and sat down across from Clara on her bed. "I wanted to discuss your leaving again. And before you say anything, please listen to me," Charity said, raising her eyebrows at Clara, waiting for her to agree not to interrupt.

Clara sighed but nodded, and Charity continued. "I know you think your work is done here, but that simply isn't true. You're the glue that holds us all together, Clara. Your cooking, your kindness to Clayton and Edrick and the Morrises. You make the ranch as a whole brighter and happier to live and work at. And speaking of them, what about the Morrises? Are you just going to abandon them after spending all that time getting to know them? And haven't you noticed how Billy looks at you? He's quite a handsome man, and he'd make an excellent husband. Why not give him a chance? After all, you're already in love with his son. And then you could be a happy family and we could all live on the ranch together. Wouldn't that be wonderful? Oh please, Clara, say you'll consider it."

Clara looked at her cousin and admired her seemingly relentless optimism, wishing she had the same gift. While it was true that she thought Billy handsome, she couldn't imagine herself with the man in any kind of romantic relationship. He was kind and warm and strong, but he wasn't the man for her. Billy was still pining for his wife, and Clara did not want to play second fiddle to the ghost of a lost love, even if it meant winning Jacob in the bargain.

"Billy certainly is attractive, and I won't deny my affection for Jacob, but I don't see myself becoming part of their family. Truthfully, Clara, I think I need to make a change in my life. If I stayed here with you, I would be falling into your life rather than creating my own. I need to go back to New York. I've decided to start a charity, using the funds my parents left me to take care of crippled and disadvantaged boys like Jacob. I want to do something with my life, Charity, something that helps children. And I don't think I can do that out here. At least not to my satisfaction. I need to challenge myself."

"But you have challenged yourself! You came all the way out here with me, convinced we wouldn't even survive the journey. And now look at you, practically running the ranch."

Clara smiled sadly at the compliment. "Yes, but the point is to keep on challenging myself. If I stay here, Charity, I'll be an obstacle to you and Clayton, preventing you from ever fully getting to know each other because you'll always be worried about me. I need to be my own woman, and take care of myself. Don't you understand?"

Charity nodded as if she understood, but Clara didn't miss the tears trickling down her cousin's cheeks. "But you're my best friend. I'll miss you so much. You're all the family I have left, Clara. If you leave, I'll never see you again."

. . . .

Clara sighed loudly and stood up to sit next to Charity on her bed. She wrapped an arm around her best friend's shoulder. "That isn't true. I will come and visit you and you can do the same with me. Being separated by distance does not mean our friendship will fall apart, or that we'll stop being family. But... I need to live my life, Charity. I cannot just disappear into yours. I have been so safe my whole life, from the moment my mother and father died. Maybe because they died. I need to stop depending on others for my destiny. Does that make any sense?"

Charity sniffled and nodded, "Yes, yes, I suppose it does. I will miss you, Clara. I will miss you so much, but if this is what you need to do to be happy, then go home. Go home and get what you need from this life. Clayton and Edrick and I will manage. You've helped me so much, and focused so much on me. Now, you need to do the same for yourself. Go home and help boys like Jacob and be happy."

CHAPTER 11

Clara stayed up long after Charity fell asleep that night, lying in bed looking at the ceiling and thinking about what her cousin had said. It warmed her heart that her friend thought she was the glue that held the ranch together, and she did love the idea of living on the ranch as one happy family with Clayton and Charity always close by. The problem was that it wasn't possible.

Clara couldn't marry Billy, and the only other single man on the ranch was Edrick, who had only recently warmed to her, and only to the degree that he warned her away from danger and occasionally complimented her on her cooking. She was sure that his echoing of Charity and Clayton at dinner that night had been a blip, the result of silent pressure, perhaps a swift kick under the table from his brother to say something kind to her.

And while she wouldn't deny that Edrick was devilishly handsome, Clara feared he suffered from the same problems as Billy: still pining for his deceased wife, except that he also blamed himself for her death. He had experienced so much tragedy in his life for a 35-year-old. Just the day before, Charity had told Clara that Edrick had been present at his mother's death. Mrs. Ashmore had collapsed from the heat one summer day three years ago and fainted in his arms. Edrick had been carrying her back to the ranch house when she died, and Charity told Clara that Edrick had been beside himself at her death, blaming himself for not doing more to save her.

He was a lost, angry man, full of grief. While Clara found him intriguing, she doubted they would ever feel anything for each other besides uncomfortable respect and the slight attraction that was natural when a woman came into contact with a man who looked like Edrick. No, it was best if she moved back to New York and focused on her charitable work. Letting Edrick Ashmore occupy her thoughts was a waste of her mental capacity.

Clara decided to begin the next day focusing solely on Charity's wedding and her plans to return to New York. With that in mind, she fell asleep, looking forward to her early morning walk, which she hoped would serve to clear any lingering cobwebs from her head.

"I'm walking over to the Morrises, but I should be back in time to prepare supper," Clara told Charity as she finished packing the small basket of food for Billy and Jacob.

"Take your time, Clara. I'm happy to do the cooking for one day to give you more time with them, especially since you're leaving so soon," Charity said.

Clara nodded, glad her cousin was coming to terms with her leaving for New York after the wedding. She had sent one of the ranch hands to purchase her ticket, and now that the piece of paper was safely stored in her trunk, it all felt suddenly real. She really was leaving.

Outside, the weather was warm, the smell of flowers and pollen heavy in the air as Clara walked over to Jacob and Billy's home. In New York the weather would still be cold and wet, the summer blooms not due for at least another month. Clara would miss the easy sunshine and heat of Texas and the feeling of the sun on her back as she walked the fields.

As Clara approached the house, she noticed to her surprise that Edrick's horse, Herbert, a large, dark brown stallion, was tied up outside. But what could he possibly be doing there?

Her question was answered a moment later when she walked up the porch steps and stood in the doorway, shocked at the scene before her. Edrick was seated at the kitchen table with Jacob, playing some sort of game with rocks and sticks. They were both eating the crisp, red apples Clara recognized from the fruit storage in the main ranch house's barn, and Edrick was laughing, his eyes closed, and his head thrown back as he guffawed.

"Miss Clara, you're here! Mr. Edrick has been showing me a game we can play outside. Would you like to try?" Jacob asked, turning to beam at Clara.

Edrick immediately sat up straighter when he realized she was in the doorway, but she noticed that his smile didn't fade. She found him even more handsome with a grin on his face.

"That sounds lovely, Jacob. And where did you

get that apple?" Clara asked, entering the room and taking a seat across from Jacob at the table. She resisted the urge to look at Edrick to her left, fearful that if she caught another glance of his smiling face, she would never stop herself staring.

"Mr. Edrick brought it for me! He's kind like you. He said he wanted to make sure I'm well fed so I can grow big and strong like him," Jacob said, turning and looking adoringly at the man. She saw a blush begin to creep up Edrick's neck at Jacob's praise.

"And it looks as though you have brought provisions of your own," Edrick said in a low, quiet voice, nodding his head at the basket at her feet.

"Oh! Yes!" Clara said, having entirely forgotten her purpose in coming. "Yes, I've brought them some more preserves and corn bread, and a bit of dried meat as well."

Clara stood up and walked over to the stove at the far end of the room, busying herself with putting the food away and hoping that a little distance from Edrick would allow her mind to quiet. She had never felt this affected by him, but seeing him smiling and playing with Jacob, treating the boy with the kindness she had so begged him to show the Morris family, overwhelmed her. Edrick had listened to her. He might not have appreciated her suggestion at dinner a few nights before but in the end, he had taken her words on board and made them a reality. He was not at all the stoic, silent, angry man she thought he was. He had layers, complicated facets to him that showed him to be more than met the eye. She was intrigued.

"Perhaps I should go," he addressed Clara's back, startling her. Clara turned to find Edrick close enough to touch and looking at her intently.

"No! No, of course you shouldn't. You must stay. Look how happy you are making Jacob," Clara said, nodding her head at the little boy who was happily playing with the sticks and rocks on the table and biting into another of the apples Edrick had brought him.

Edrick turned to look, and she didn't miss the strange combination of contentment and grief that briefly flashed across his face before his features once again settled into an easy smile. What about the boy could be saddening him? Yes, Jacob was crippled, but at that moment, his disability wasn't affecting him. He was playing the same as any child, enjoying his life with the carefree whimsy particular to one his age.

Edrick turned back to Clara and nodded. "Yes, well, if you like, I will stay. Perhaps we could take the boy outside and you could teach him more of his letters."

"How do you know I'm teaching him his letters?" Clara asked, confused. She didn't remember mentioning that at any of the meals they had eaten together recently.

Edrick paused, looking awkward. "Oh...um, well...I was passing this way yesterday and... happened to see you two writing in the dirt. In passing. On my horse."

Clara nearly giggled at how pained Edrick looked while admitting that. But rather than torture the man further, she moved away from the stove, allowing him a moment to return to his normal, non-stuttering self. "Alright, Jacob, let us adjourn to the dirt and continue learning the alphabet!"

Clara helped Jacob out of his chair and held his hand in hers as they made their way outside. Edrick followed behind, grabbing two sticks off the table and handing them to Clara once they reached the porch steps.

Clara thanked him and settled herself in the dirt just in front of the house. She and Jacob were now writing small phrases like "I ate" or "You ran" and so she began sketching out some of these in the dirt while Jacob watched with rapt attention. When she had finished, she asked him to copy them and then she went to sit on the edge of the step leading to the house, next to Edrick, watching while Jacob worked.

"It is very kind of you to teach him, Clara," Edrick said, determined not to look at her and instead focusing on the boy as he bent over and moved the stick in long, clean lines in the dirt.

Clara shrugged, "It is a necessary skill, reading."

Edrick nodded, and for a few minutes they sat in silence, watching Jacob work diligently in front of them to trace the letters out in the dirt.

Clara helped Jacob learn a few more phrases, and by then the sun was high in the sky and it was time for Jacob and Billy to take their afternoon meal together. She knew it was a sacred time for them, a chance to catch up on the day so far. Although Charity had told Clara she was more than welcome to stay out while she cooked, Clara wanted to head back to the ranch house and give the Morrises their privacy.

"Jacob, I'll be back tomorrow morning," Clara said, stooping down to hug the boy. Clara always made sure to show him physical affection whenever she visited, whether it was a hug or a simple running of her hand through his hair. Billy Morris was not a physically affectionate man by nature, and Clara worried that without his mother, Jacob would be shown little of the hugs and kisses and caresses that had made Clara sure as a child that she was loved and wanted and important. She wanted to make sure that Jacob knew he was all of those things and more.

She didn't miss the look Edrick gave her as she stood up from the dirt and brushed her dress off, a cloud of dirt billowing out as she shook out her skirts. He was looking at her with admiration, an intense approbation that colored her cheeks and made her warm to her very core.

"I can ride you back to the ranch house, if you like," Edrick invited when Clara returned from collecting her shawl from inside the house.

"Oh! But that would be so inconvenient for you. You must have so many things to attend to."

Edrick shook his head. "It would be my pleasure to accompany you back to the ranch house, Clara." She loved the way her name sounded on his lips, like a reverent benediction.

"Alright. Yes. But you'll have to help me onto

the horse. I'm afraid I am not a very skilled horsewoman." That comment earned her another smile from Edrick. She'd seen more grins from the man that morning than in all the weeks she'd lived in River Creek up to then. It was a miracle. One she couldn't help but attribute to Jacob.

Edrick led Clara over to his horse. He untied the reins from the hitching post and then he turned to her, and wordlessly wrapped his hands around her waist and hoisted her into the saddle. Clara felt the tingle of his hands on her even after Edrick removed them, and to her surprise, she felt bereft at the loss of contact.

Edrick jumped into the saddle behind her and flicked the reins, signaling Herbert to set off at a slow pace. Clara grabbed onto the horn of the saddle for support. "Thank you for your suggestion to visit the Morrises," he said in her ear as they passed fields of grass tinged with gold under the sunlight.

"You're welcome. You and Jacob seemed to get along quite well. He looked so happy playing with you."

Clara heard Edrick clear his throat behind her and then in a slightly gruff voice he said, "He's the same age my child would have been, had my wife lived. I always imagined we were having a boy. I wanted to name him John, after my father."

Clara's heart broke at the huskiness she heard in Edrick's throat, as though he was holding back strong emotion: grief, no doubt. To lose not only his wife but also his unborn child must have been heartbreaking.

"I'm so sorry for your loss, Edrick. You would have been a good father, and I imagine you must have been an excellent husband."

Edrick scoffed. "Yes, well, not excellent enough to save my wife."

Clara turned to face him, not caring that the motion made her momentarily fearful she would fall from the saddle and hit her head the way she had so often imagined doing during those fearful first few days on the train. She needed to comfort the man, to remind him that his wife's death was an accident and not his fault.

"It wasn't your fault, Edrick. Unfortunately, women die while pregnant or in childbirth quite frequently. It is one of life's great tragedies, that the act our bodies spend a lifetime preparing for can also be the death of us. But it is never anyone's fault, least of all the men who love us. Don't blame yourself, Edrick."

Clara looked into Edrick's eyes for a moment, saw the shock and awe in them, and the gratitude, too. She turned around, facing forward and felt the brush of his hands on her hips as he adjusted his grip on the reins. A silent thank you. Together, they rode the rest of the way to the house in the comfortable silence of two people who know and understand each other.

CHAPTER 12

The day of the wedding approached quickly, and then it was upon them. Clara and Charity were frantically putting the finishing touches to the wedding dress and ensuring that Charity's hair would stay secure in its tasteful but complicated braid.

"You look beautiful," Clara told Charity when they had finished dressing her. The simple pink dress that Clara had sewn for her brought out the rosiness of Charity's skin and accentuated the golden highlights in her blonde hair. She was a vision, an angel, and Clara was so pleased that she was able to see her cousin so happy. Charity hadn't stopped beaming from the moment she had announced her engagement, and Clara had a feeling that those smiles would continue through the wedding and all the years of their marriage. She had never seen a happier couple.

"And so do you, Clara. I can't believe you managed to make these dresses in such a short time," Charity beamed, smoothing her hands over the soft fabric of her dress. Clara had rushed to town the day after Charity's announcement that she was to wed, to buy bolts of fabric, needles, scissors and the necessary accoutrement to create a wedding dress she felt worthy of her cousin and best friend. She had also sewn herself a gown, a simple blue and white affair with lace detailing and pockets large enough to hold the handkerchief she knew she would need to dry her happy tears during the ceremony.

"Yes, well, I wasn't a seamstress all those years for nothing!" Clara said, smiling at Charity. She took her cousin's hand in hers and led her out of their house and across the field to the main ranch house. Edrick and Clayton were outside, dressed in their best suits. Clayton wore a new waistcoat of fine grey fabric, matching trousers and a fine, white cotton shirt that Clara had sewn for him. He certainly looked dashing, but it was Edrick that Clara could not keep her eyes off of.

The tight, light blue cotton shirt he wore accentuated his muscular build. The black of his waistcoat brought out the depth of color in his hair. He was chatting about something to Clayton, and laughing, and Clara's breath caught as his head tilted back and he opened his mouth and guffawed. Clara decided that she liked Edrick best when he was laughing. His face opened up and he appeared ten years younger, loosening the grief and hardship that had lined his eyes and mouth.

"How handsome he is!" Charity whispered as they approached the men and, for a moment, Clara thought she meant Edrick. She was about to whisper her agreement when she realized that, of course, her cousin meant her betrothed, Clayton.

The last few days and the numerous interactions with Edrick had thoroughly confused Clara; suddenly, Edrick was kind and talkative and helpful. The antithesis of who he was when they had first met. Clara didn't know what to think of him now and she didn't know how to interpret the feeling of butterflies at every glance.

"You both look beautiful," Clayton said, coming to loop Charity's arm in his and lead her to the horse and buggy they were taking to town. Clara and Edrick walked behind them, silent and lost in contemplation, each wondering what the other was thinking.

The ride to town was short, and so was the wedding. Most of the citizens of River Creek were busy with their ranching and farming, leaving them little time to attend a wedding. Therefore, the crowd at the church was sparse, and the service quick. Neither Charity nor Clayton seemed to mind, besotted as they were with each other. They had not stopped smiling from the moment they entered the church. They gave each other looks of deep affection and longing all through the service. The kiss they exchanged after their vows was chaste but full of feeling, and it was this that made Clara tear up, because when Charity pulled away, she had a look of pure, incandescent happiness on her face.

"Well, that was lovely, but I think I shall go for a walk now that the service is over. It's far too beautiful a day to spend inside, don't you think?" Clara said as they left the church and walked back onto the crowded main street. She knew that Clayton and Charity wanted some time alone, but the weather was also truly fine, and she wanted a long walk before returning to the ranch house to prepare the evening meal.

"Are you sure, Clara?" Charity asked in a tone of voice that told her she was more than happy to be left alone with her new husband.

"Yes," Clara replied firmly.

"I think I will go check on the cattle," Edrick said as he came to stand next to Clara. "See how they're getting on in the heat." It was not overly warm outside, but Clara suspected that like her, Edrick wanted to give the newlyweds some time alone.

"Splendid. Well, shall we all meet for dinner this evening at the ranch house, then? Charity and I can take the carriage back," Clayton asked, looking from one face to the next. Nods and words of farewell were exchanged. Clara and Edrick were alone, Clayton and Charity having walked off toward a saloon in town for a celebratory drink.

"Might I walk with you a way, Clara?" Edrick turned to her and asked. Clara nodded, secretly glad for the company. As happy as she was for Charity, now that the wedding was over, her departure to New York was approaching and she found herself sad at the prospect of leaving River Creek. Days as beautiful as this made her realize just how much she would miss what had so quickly become her home.

"Yes, that would be lovely, Edrick." They set off toward the ranch, falling into an easy rhythm, Edrick walking slightly ahead of Clara. Clara relished the feel of the sun on her, even taking off her hat and allowing the rays to warm her face. She could sacrifice a few freckles for the sensation of the delicious warmth on her cheeks.

They were nearing the ranch property line when Edrick suddenly slowed down until Clara was beside him. He broke the easy silence that had colored the last twenty minutes or so. "I am very sorry that you will be leaving soon, Clara. Your presence at the ranch will be missed by us all."

Clara saw genuine sadness and regret in his eyes, and it mirrored her own feelings. "Yes, well, it is for the best, I believe." But even as she said it, Clara wondered if that was really true.

Though the prospect of forging out on her own in New York was exciting, in the last few days she had come to appreciate the way of life in River Creek. Long days of walks and playing with Jacob and cooking, nights reading and sewing and chatting, and the presence of so many kind people made her loathe to leave. But her ticket was booked for the day after tomorrow, and her trunk was nearly packed.

Edrick made a non-committal noise as he opened the gate for Clara, allowing her to enter the property ahead of him. They walked a bit further together, and as they neared the first field of cattle, Edrick turned to her, his face presenting the familiar scowl, "I must see to the cows, but I shall see you for dinner, yes?"

Clara nodded and continued on toward the creek. She needed the gentle tinkling sound of the water moving over the rocks to calm her mind. It would be her last opportunity to hear that blissful sound, and she wanted to soak up as much of it as she could, to savor the vision of the cool blue water contrasting with the packed red dirt of the riverbed, the sunshine at her back and the whole day ahead of her. Her last in this amazing place that continued to surprise and excite her.

CHAPTER 13

Clara had walked for a good hour by the time she decided to rest. It was the furthest she had ever walked down the creek, and she could no longer see the fields or the ranchers' houses behind her. Her surroundings were perfectly peaceful and quiet and undisturbed.

Up ahead was a flat rock that invited her to rest awhile. Clara made her way toward it. She was thirsty and would appreciate a long drink of water. Before venturing into the water to satisfy her thirst, she needed to rest her legs. Although she had grown much stronger over the past weeks, thanks in no small part to the walking, she had never walked such a distance.

Clara approached the rock without thinking,

exhaustion distracting her from the slickness of the rocks at her feet. The day was warm and dry, but the spray from the creek had reached the rocks, and Clara's foot slipped on a small stone. She leaned to the right to catch her balance, but then her left foot shot out in front of her, and she was falling, falling, falling, sliding down the side of the riverbed and landing feet-first in the water. Clara scrambled to stand but found that her ankle was lodged between two rocks, the rushing water preventing her from escaping. She struggled, growing frantic, looking for anything that would give her the leverage she needed to extricate herself.

Looking up, she saw a branch growing out of the walls of the riverbed, and she grabbed onto it, pulling against it as she tried to free her leg from its trap. Clara did not realize that this branch was growing from beneath a large rock at the top of the creek bed. Her weight on it soon dislodged the rock which landed on her ankle, trapping her in the water and causing a sharp, biting pain up her lower leg.

Tears began to run down Clara's face as she struggled to free herself. The more she wiggled her ankle this way and that, the more the pain rushed up her limbs and to her head, making her dizzy and even more fearful of falling over.

I just need to rest for a moment, and then I'll try again, Clara told herself. She sat carefully. She let the water soak through her newly sewn dress, not caring when it soaked through her petticoats and caused her to shiver despite the sun still shining down on her. She was simply grateful for the chance to rest.

But Clara found that even after she had rested, she couldn't stand. The strength had gone out of her legs, trapping her in a seated position as the water continued to flow all around her. As the sun moved in the sky from high noon to the lingering rays of early evening, Clara sat, wondering how she was ever going to get herself out of this mess. All she had wanted was a peaceful walk to clear her mind and allow her to take in the scenery she would miss so much. Now she was trapped in the river, growing colder with every moment, the pain in her ankle shooting up and down her leg and forcing her to take deep, steadying breaths to keep from crying out. She was trapped and no one was coming to save her.

"Where is Clara?" Edrick asked, looking around

the ranch house. He had just returned from finishing his chores in the horse barn and expected to find Clara at the stove, preparing the evening meal.

Charity and Clayton were sitting at the table drinking coffee and staring deep into each other's eyes. Edrick ignored the heavy feeling that seeing their love caused in his chest. He was happy for his brother, but that happiness did not cancel out the jealousy he felt over Clayton having found the love of his life while he was alone, without a wife or child or anyone to care for.

Charity tore herself away from her husband's gaze and looked up. "She isn't here. I assumed she was still on her walk."

Edrick pondered that, walking to the kitchen and pouring a cup of coffee from the carafe on the stove. "She does enjoy a long stroll, but do you not think it odd she isn't back by now? It's late afternoon. She's been gone for hours."

"Let us wait a few more minutes for her to return. She is leaving the day after tomorrow, after all. Perhaps she fancied a stroll about the property, a last chance to view it all before she has to say goodbye," Clayton suggested.

Edrick took a seat at the table and sipped

slowly at his coffee. The uneasiness that had hit him the moment he realized that Clara was absent was not easing in the slightest. Admittedly, the reasons Clayton and Charity gave for her absence were perfectly reasonable, but they did not sit well with him. Something was wrong. He could feel it.

After thirty minutes without a sign of Clara, Edrick jumped up from his chair. "It has been four and a half hours since the wedding, and she is still not back. I know the girl appreciates a bit of outdoor exercise, but this is a long walk even for her. She's always back by this time, chopping vegetables or preserving fruit or doing whatever other magic she does in the kitchen. That she isn't here is a bad sign. Something must have happened. Clayton, we need to find her."

Charity's brow creased with worry as Edrick spoke, and he could see her growing more and more upset with every second that passed. Her wedding haze was evaporating as the true gravity of the situation hit her. "Oh dear...you're right. What could have happened to her? It's nearly dark—she could be in danger and we'd never even know!"

Clayton stood and put an arm around his wife.

"Don't worry, Charity. We'll find her. Won't we, Edrick?"

Edrick grunted in response, not bothering to answer his brother fully as he walked out the house in the direction of the riverbed. If she had encountered a misfortune, it would be on those rocks. He could feel it in his bones. He was already kicking himself for waiting even thirty minutes before searching for her. Edrick picked up his pace, mapping the fastest route to the riverbed. He wouldn't be too late to save yet another woman left in his care. Not this time.

Charity stayed behind while Clayton and Edrick hurried toward the creek. Edrick tried to tamper the panic rising in his chest with each passing minute as the sun set and traversing the ground became more treacherous, even by the light of their lanterns.

They jogged next to the creek, shining the lanterns onto the fast-moving water and searching for Clara. After a half an hour of careful searching, there was still no sign of her. Edrick was about ready to growl in frustration and let lose the panic he felt, when he caught sight of blue fabric snagged on a branch just below them. Moving his lantern far above his head, he shifted the light, shining it directly below him, past the fabric and onto the figure of Clara, her arms wrapped around her shins and her head buried between her knees. Her shoulders were shaking with quiet, gentle sobs.

"Clara?" Edrick called and her head shot up. Even in the dim light he could see the tracks of many tears on her beautiful face. She looked exhausted and scared, but when she recognized his voice, he saw the fear in her eyes recede.

"Edrick? Is that you? Oh, thank the Lord! You must help me! My ankle is stuck between two rocks and I can't get up, and a rock fell and further trapped my leg. I've been like this for hours."

Edrick handed his lantern to his brother, along with his hat and cloak. "Shine the light directly down so I can see what I'm doing. I'm going to go down and see if I can move the rocks that are trapping her," he instructed Clayton.

Edrick carefully climbed down into the river, the water quickly soaking through his trousers and leather boots. He stooped down to assess the damage and winced slightly at the odd angle of Clara's ankle. It might not be broken, but it was definitely badly sprained and would take some time to heal. It was trapped between two large rocks embedded in the river bed, which meant that moving them enough to free Clara's ankle would take some time and effort. The rock that had fallen on her would be much easier to remove; it looked to weigh no more than the average bale of damp hay, and Edrick was confident he could move it and slide it to the side of the creek bed.

"Alright, Clara, I'm going to very carefully lift this rock off you, then I'm going to move the rocks trapping your ankle. The release of pressure is going to cause quite a bit of pain, but I know you're strong. Take a deep breath now and relax. If you tense, the pain will be worse." Edrick watched as Clara inhaled and exhaled, preparing herself for the discomfort. She nodded to show that she was ready, and Edrick crouched down to grip the rock crushing her right leg, before slowly and carefully lifting the large rock.

Clara cried out, clutching her ankle and shin, clearly in pain. Edrick made quick work of moving the rock to the side before rushing back to her. "It's alright, Clara. It's just the feeling coming back to your leg after so long under pressure. Breathe through the pain. It will get better, I swear it." Clara nodded, tears falling down her cheeks as Edrick stood up, steadying his footing among the rocks and pebbles before stooping down to free her ankle.

"Clayton, a bit more light down here, please," he called, and Clayton shifted the lanterns so that bright beams of light shone down on the rocks trapping Clara's foot. They were pressing against her ankle, no doubt rubbing at the skin and bones. Edrick winced thinking about the pain they must be causing Clara, but that only motivated him to help her, to use his strength to free her from the river. Edrick squatted down and grasped one of the rocks, using all his weight to lift it and push it to the side. He grunted with the effort, the veins in his neck growing more pronounced as he took a deep breath and slowly hauled the rock a few inches over, placing it on top of the other rock he had moved.

Clara breathed a sigh of relief at the release of the weight, "Thank you."

Edrick returned to her side and stooped down again, his eyes looking into Clara's. "Now, I'm going to see if I can lift you up and out of the riverbed, Clara. Are you ready?" Edrick asked, peering down at her.

"Yes, yes, I'm ready."

Edrick gently placed his hands under Clara's

armpits, using the strength of his legs and arms to lift her. She bit back a cry of pain as her ankle moved position, dangling in the air for a moment. Then she was in Edrick's arms and he was lifting her out of the riverbed and to safety.

Clara could feel her ankle throbbing with pain as Edrick carried her all the way back to the house. At some point she fell asleep, exhausted by the ordeal. Clayton covered her with Edrick's coat. Clara could have stayed like that forever, safe in Edrick's strong arms, were it not for the shriek from Charity when Edrick walked into the house.

CHAPTER 14

"You found her! Is she alright?" Charity called out, waking Clara as she rushed at her still nestled in Edrick's arms in the doorway.

"She was in the riverbed, her ankle trapped under and between some rocks," Edrick said as he carried her through the main living area and into his room, placing her on the bed. Charity followed close behind, anxiously peering over his shoulder as he adjusted the pillows at Clara's back.

Edrick stepped aside and Charity rushed forward, anxiety clear in her eyes. Clara winced with pain when her cousin sat down next to her on the bed, the jostling causing her ankle to move in just such a way as to cause a burst of pain that momentarily blurred her vision. Charity noticed the wince. "Oh, I'm so sorry!" she shrieked, leaping up and backing away until she was against the wall.

"It's alright, Charity," Clara said, adjusting her leg until she was comfortable again. She saw Edrick exit the room but did not have time to consider his leaving before her cousin was back at her side.

"Is it painful?" she whispered.

Clara nodded, "Yes, but that is beside the point. I should be the one apologizing, not you. I'm sure this isn't quite how you imagined your wedding night. You're worrying about me."

"Nonsense!" Charity said, stepping forward, hands on her hips. "Clayton and I have the rest of our married lives together. Right now, I'm just glad you're all right. What happened? You were gone for absolutely hours, and you're soaking wet."

Clara explained that she had slipped on the rocks, fallen and been unable to get up, trapped in the riverbed until Edrick and Clayton found her just after dusk.

"Thank goodness for Edrick. He lifted the rocks away like they were feathers, helped me up and carried me all the way back here in his arms."

Charity nodded, "He was so worried about you. The moment he noticed you weren't in the house, he started agonizing that something bad had happened to you. I'm sorry to say that Clayton and I were too preoccupied with chatting to notice your absence. I've been so selfish, Clara. I'm so sorry. Maybe if we'd noticed you weren't here sooner, your ankle wouldn't be so sore and swollen." Charity nodded at Clara's ankle, which was indeed swollen to twice its size and turning a sickening shade of purple and blue.

"Nonsense! I should have remembered Edrick's warning about the rocks being slippery. I was just so lost in the scenery that when I went to sit down and have a rest, I didn't even think to be careful. It's so beautiful there, so peaceful and quiet. But then, I supposed that is why I was nearly sick with cold and a sprained ankle by the time someone found me. No one could hear me crying out all the way out there."

Clara was about to continue when Clayton walked into the room, interrupting them. Having heard their conversation, he walked toward Clara and said, "It's no one's fault. Clara, you slipping and falling on the rocks was an accident, simple as that. What we need to focus on is not placing blame but getting you better. That's the most important thing right this very minute."

Charity conceded his point, "That is true, my dear. Is there a doctor in town who can see to her? Someone willing to come this late at night?"

Clayton nodded, "Edrick has just saddled Herbert and is now riding to call Doctor Philips. He's taken care of us for as long as I can remember. He should be here within the hour."

"Oh no, you don't think it's broken, do you? Or sprained? Doesn't that mean I won't be able to walk?" Clara said anxiously, sitting up slightly and eyeing her ankle. It was true that it did not look as it should, but surely the swelling would go down quickly, and she would be able to put weight on it again. After all, she had a train to catch. She had plans in New York, a whole new life and a charity to start. She couldn't be stuck in River Creek!

"I think we should wait until the doctor arrives before speculating. I'm hardly experienced in medicine, unless it's to do with horses, and you are no horse, Clara. All I can tell you is that from my vantage point, the injury looks rather painful," Clayton said, giving Clara a sympathetic look.

"That it is," she said, sighing.

Clara's worst fears were confirmed when

Edrick returned with Doctor Philips in tow. He shook his head gravely as he pressed. "The good news is that it isn't broken. But it's badly sprained. You'll need to stay off your feet for at least a week if not more, and you must keep it elevated at all times."

"But...but I have a train to catch!" Clara said from her position on the bed, with Charity, Clayton and Edrick clustered around her. Doctor Phillips was standing at the foot of the bed examining her ankle, his fingers gently prodding at the bruise, but he looked up at the note of panic in her voice.

"My dear girl," he said gently, taking off his glasses and folding them before placing them in the left breast pocket of his coat. "You are young and strong and will recover easily from this injury, but only if you give yourself the time to do so. Ankles are what keep us walking and going about our daily business, and not allowing them to recover from injuries such as this is an excellent way to ensure you won't be going on any more of the long walks I've been told you favor. And you won't be able to stand for hours at the stove, either. It's in your best interest to follow my advice if you plan to keep up with such activities in the future."

Clara sighed and nodded, knowing in her heart that the doctor was right. She knew she needed to stay in River Creek to rest and recuperate. But doing so would mean missing out on her chance to return to New York. While she knew rationally that she could simply purchase another ticket once she was healed, in her mind, it felt as though the door to the life she had been dreaming of was closing. She didn't understand the warring sense of disappointment and relief she felt coursing through her veins. She was confused and tired and in pain.

"I think it best if you take some broth and then rest, my dear," Doctor Phillips said as he gathered his bag and coat. "I will check on your ankle in a few days, and I expect to hear that you've been convalescing and allowing these fine gentlemen and your dear cousin to dote on you. No walking until I see you again, do you hear me?"

"Don't worry, Doctor Phillips. We'll see to it that she gets all the rest she needs," Charity said, giving Clara a look that said don't you dare get up as she showed the doctor to the front door and back to his horse.

Clara lay back on the pillows and watched Clayton follow Charity out of the room, leaving her and Edrick alone. A moment of uneasy silence passed between them before Edrick said, "I think it best you stay here while you are convalescing," gesturing around the room. "It will be much easier to attend to you if you stay in the main ranch house rather than the smaller cabin out back."

Clara looked shocked. "Absolutely not! I'll be perfectly fine in the house at the back. If you take me there now, I can fall right asleep. This whole ordeal has been rather exhausting."

Edrick shook his head, the tone of his voice communicating that he would not accept any arguments, "Absolutely not. What if something were to happen to you in the middle of the night? What if you fell out of bed and injured yourself further? There would be no one to hear your cries or to help you. What if you needed a glass or water or some broth? There would be no one to bring it to you. No, you will stay in this room until you are fully healed. It is decided, Clara."

Clara crossed her arms and glared at the handsome man in front of her. "Okay."

CHAPTER 15

"I know you're feeling a bit restless right now, but you have to keep reminding yourself that you'll never get better unless you rest. Walking outside at the crack of dawn and hopping on one foot to see blooms is not resting," Charity chided as she stood up from where she had been sitting on the end of Clara's bed.

Clara had attempted to walk that morning, eager to see the spring blooms on the trees out front that had begun sprouting on the day she had fallen. Clara had woken before dawn, aching to see those flowers. She had taken her early wake-up as a sign that it was time to look at the tree. After all, it was before sunrise, and surely no one else would notice her brief absence from bed.

But of course, though Charity and Clayton were still asleep, Edrick was up and sitting on the porch, seemingly deep in contemplation when Clara's hobbled gait creaked on the old wood of the structure, alerting him to her presence. He had given her what she was beginning to refer to in her mind as his signature scowl, and carried her back to bed, where she had dutifully remained for the rest of the day. And now, she was still in bed, after a thorough scolding from Charity and an extracted promise not to move from her supine position until Doctor Phillips pronounced her fully healed. He was due to stop by later that day, but Clara suspected that, given that the bruise hadn't completely faded, and it still hurt to turn her ankle the few times she had tried, it was doubtful she would be given a clean bill of health.

"But I feel so useless! You're having to do all the cooking and cleaning by yourself as well as taking regular baskets to Jacob and Billy. And all I can do is sit in bed, read the Bible and rue the day I ever attempted to walk on those rocks down by the river. I haven't seen Jacob in what feels like months. What if he isn't practicing his letters? What if he's forgotten all I've taught him?"

Charity laughed and shook her head. "Clara! You've done more than your share of household tasks over the last few weeks. For once in your life, let someone else take care of things. And of course Jacob won't forget everything. He's a bright boy, and a few days without your tutelage won't do him any harm, my dear." Charity leaned down and pressed a kiss to Clara's forehead, and with that, she left the room, and Clara was once again alone with her thoughts.

Thoughts that lately had started her wondering whether she really wanted to leave River Creek after her ankle had healed, whenever that might be. The more time she spent in the house around Charity, Clayton, Edrick and Jacob, the more she realized that, although she had not expected it, Ashmore Ranch had become her home. With a makeshift family to go along with it. In fact, it felt more like home than New York City ever had. Yes, the brownstone in New York City would always hold a special place in her heart as the house in which she had grown up and had shared so many happy memories with her now deceased parents, but it was no longer her home. Perhaps it was high time she closed up the house. She had stopped feeling fond of its walls years ago. When she imagined where she wanted to go each day to hang her hat, as it were, it was not the brownstone, but the ranch house in River Creek. Clara knew she could leave the house in Alice's capable hands. She would do an excellent job managing the property for her, ensuring it was ready if guests ever visited. Clara knew she could have her affairs settled and her money rerouted to River Creek with one letter to Mr. Seymour. It was something to think about, she decided, before falling back asleep.

"Well, it's healing nicely, but I don't think you're quite out of the woods yet, I'm afraid, my dear girl. At least another few days of rest and elevation are needed before you're back to your regular walks and time in the kitchen," Doctor Phillips said to Clara later that day upon finishing his examination of her ankle.

Even though Clara had suspected as much, she still couldn't help feeling disappointment at the doctor's words. She felt more trapped than ever and wanted more than ever to be outside, enjoying the fresh spring air and playing with Jacob in the dirt, instead of lying in bed. She could smell the blooms on the breeze blowing in through the window, and she ached to feel the sunshine on her face. She so longed for her normal routine of cooking and cleaning and walking and spending time with her family outside the room that had become her prison.

Knowing she wouldn't be free for at least a few more days thoroughly depressed her. After Doctor Phillips left, she begged to be left alone, and immediately took another long nap. When Charity came in later, she found her still asleep, which was unusual for Clara, even while convalescing.

"I've never seen her sleep so much! Not even after her mother died," Charity divulged to Clayton after closing the door to Edrick's room and joining her husband who was leaning on the porch railing, looking at the sunset.

"Leave her be for a while, darling. I'm sure she's just tired after the doctor's visit. Let's let her sleep a bit longer and then you can wake her up for supper." Clayton hugged Charity to his side, but even the embrace didn't quiet her nerves.

Charity had a right to be nervous, because even after she slaved over the stew made from the recipe booklet Clara had gifted them for their wedding, when she presented Clara with the bowl of steaming stew, she refused it.

"I'm not hungry," she said sleepily, rolling over on the bed with what Charity suspected were tears running down her cheeks.

"But, Clara, you need to eat. You need your strength if you're going to heal."

Clara rolled over enough for her voice not to be muffled by the pillows. "With all due respect, Charity, please leave me alone, and take the stew with you."

Charity was about to walk around the bed and crouch down in front of Clara, hoping to talk some sense into her when she decided against it. Clara was a grown woman who knew her needs, and if she wanted to rest and not eat, then that's exactly what Charity would give her the space and time to do.

But it didn't mean she wouldn't worry about Clara. She crept back to the kitchen, set the tray by the stove and collapsed into a chair across from Clayton who was sitting at the table, waiting for her to eat.

"Eat! Please! Someone in this house has to," she whispered, picking up her own spoon and digging into the stew. It wasn't as good as Clara's, but

Clayton slurped it up just the same, no doubt worried about offending his wife if he did otherwise.

Edrick came in a moment later, sat at the table and scooped up a bite of stew. "This is delicious, Charity. Real good, rib-sticking food. Right, Clayton?" he said, and though Charity knew Edrick was complimenting her to cheer her up, she smiled nevertheless and thanked him.

"How is Clara doing today?" he asked as he continued eating. Charity's shoulders slumped in relief, thankful for the opportunity to vent her frustrations.

"She won't eat! She has refused two meals and she's slept through most of the day. She seemed happy enough this morning, but after Doctor Phillips left, she wilted like a dead flower. I know she's a creature of habit and this is a definite disruption of her routine, but I've never seen her so unhappy. I don't know how to help her," Charity said, wringing her hands on the kitchen table.

Clayton reached over and captured Charity's hand in his, squeezing it in comfort. "Did she mention anything to you about what specifically she missed from her routine?" he asked.

Charity nodded and wiped a tear from her eye,

"Yes. She said she was missing Jacob, said she was worried he would forget everything she'd taught him while they were apart. And she missed cooking and walking, but I don't think we can allow her to do that until she's healed. It's too much strain on her ankle."

Edrick nodded and put his spoon down, lacing his fingers under his chin. "You're correct about the cooking and cleaning, but I reckon I have a way to get Jacob to the house without causing him too much strain. Why don't I bring him here in a few days once he's recovered from the last trip?"

Charity sat up straighter and nodded, "Oh yes! Yes, that's perfect! Oh Edrick, thank you so much. You have no idea how much this will help her."

Edrick blushed slightly and looked down, suddenly bashful, "It's nothing. Just trying to keep the peace here."

Charity didn't miss the subtle elbowing Clayton gave Edrick when she started gathering the empty bowls of stew a few minutes later.

CHAPTER 16

"We should be back in time for supper. I can't imagine the errands taking that long, but are you sure you'll be able to care for Clara? How will you feed her?" Charity asked a few days later as she laced her bonnet and adjusted the sleeves of her gown.

She and Clayton had planned an outing into town, partly at Edrick's insistence. "You two need to spend some time alone together without worrying about Clara," he had told them the night before. When Charity had attempted to argue, Edrick had scowled the way he knew intimidated Clara, and the facial expression had shocked Charity into submission.

"I'm sure Edrick has everything under control,

darling," Clayton said, winking at Edrick over Charity's shoulder. Edrick held in the smirk he could feel threatening to burst on his cheeks, intent on not letting Clara know that he had a plan up his sleeve.

He and Clayton had also spoken the previous evening before supper and decided that what Clayton and Charity needed was a day in town, and what Clara needed was a day of not being doted on. "She's used to being the main woman of the house, of taking care of all of us rather than the other way around. Perhaps a day where she doesn't feel like such a convalescent would be a good thing," Clayton observed as they walked the ranch after supper.

"Yes. Yes, I believe you're right," Edrick said, nodding and already putting together a plan in his head.

"And if I am being perfectly honest, I need some time alone with Charity. She's been so worried about Clara that we've barely spoken about the future and about what she wants for her life in River Creek. An outing to town and the long walk it would entail would give me time to discuss such things with her."

"Then it is decided. Tomorrow, you will take

Charity out and I will give Clara opportunity to think about something other than her ankle." And indeed, that was exactly what Edrick planned to do. Although Edrick also had a more selfish reason for taking over the care of Clara for the day: he wanted to spend some time alone with her.

Edrick had been taking care of his daily duties at the ranch since Clara's dark day, before visiting Clara in the afternoons. He kept her updated on the goings on on the ranch each day, shared funny stories about Charity and Clayton being so besotted with each other that they walked into walls and tripped over the floor, so focused were they on looking deep into each other's eyes. The laughs these stories elicited from Clara gave Edrick life, and made him feel like perhaps he was not quite as dead inside as he had thought. Being around Clara, he forgot that his wife and mother were gone, and that his unborn child would never see the light of day. With Clara, Edrick forgot that he was a broken man.

A woman who made him feel like that deserved everything he could give her, including soup. And that was what Edrick began making as soon as Charity and Clayton left. Though he had never cooked in his life, coffee aside, Edrick had observed his mother in the kitchen often enough as a child to be somewhat familiar with a stove. He knew where the knives and spoons and pots were kept and could vaguely remember adding salt to the soup when his mother was called away into the fields. But he was a smart man, and surely if he could tame a horse and herd sixty cattle, he could make a simple meal. He set about making a beef broth the way his mother used to make for him when he was ill. The main ingredients were a ham hock, water, pepper, salt, and a bit of cornmeal for thickener. All of which he now had sitting before him on the table. It couldn't be too difficult, could it?

Three hours and two abandoned, half-cooked pans of broth later, Edrick realized that what Clara did in the kitchen every day was nothing less than pure, unfathomable magic. He had no idea how she did it. What he had come up with from his endeavors resembled nothing so much as congealed yellow porridge with a somewhat mysterious flavor. But it was all the food he had for her, and so he would serve it, hoping that her surprise over a man taking over the kitchen would shock her taste buds into numbness.

"Clara? I'm about to bring your lunch in,"

Edrick said, knocking on the door to let her know he was about to enter. Edrick brought in the tray on which he had placed a cup of lukewarm coffee, a bowl of the infamous broth, and a half-stale bread roll he had found tucked away in the pantry.

"Oh my! You cooked for me!" Clara exclaimed, sitting up in bed and marveling at the spread in front of her. "I can't believe it. Did you make this just for me?"

Edrick shrugged nonchalantly. "It was nothing." He watched with bated breath as Clara took the spoon, dipped it in the yellowish concoction and brought it to her lips. Her eyes went from wonder to confusion, and then they closed, and her face contorted briefly, her nostrils flaring as they might had they caught wind of a foul odor.

"It is…it is…very delicious. Like nothing I have ever tasted before," Clara said, putting the spoon down.

Edrick couldn't hold it in any longer, and his laughter burst forth, a large guffaw tumbling out of his mouth as he replayed the scene of Clara's face as she tasted the soup. "By interesting, do you mean vile? Because that is what I felt it was when I tasted it moments ago."

Clara's eyes widened in surprise, and then she

too began laughing, and it made Edrick's heart feel so light that he wouldn't have been surprised if it floated right out of his chest. Clara laughing was the most beautiful sight in the world; her face opening up, her cheeks growing pink and her perfectly bowed mouth letting forth giggles that sounded like the chants of an angel.

"It is delicious. I love it because you made it for me. Thank you, Edrick. It was so incredibly kind of you, and as evidence of my gratitude, I shall eat the whole bowl."

"Please don't feel obliged. The bread roll could surely satisfy you until Charity returns and can make you something proper," Edrick said, now feeling slightly embarrassed at the compliment.

Clara held out her hand, shooing away his apology. "Nonsense! I cannot wait to finish it. Now, either sit and watch me eat or be gone and continue with your kitchen experiments."

Edrick laughed and decided to stay. He talked and kept Clara company as she finished her meal, making occasional groans and appreciative noises that made him laugh so hard his sides hurt. Edrick couldn't remember the last time he had laughed like that. This woman; she truly was a marvel.

"Now, I have another surprise for you," Edrick admitted when he returned to the room after clearing Clara's dishes and setting them on the sink for washing. "I do need to leave the house briefly to fetch it, but I promise it will be well worth the wait."

"Oh, Edrick, you've done more than enough for me today. Go back to the ranch and your duties. I will be fine, honestly. I'm quite tired out; perhaps I'll have a rest," Clara said. She wasn't used to being treated so kindly by anyone other than Charity or her maids, and this kind of attention from a man, especially Edrick, made her feel both excited and nervous.

"Nonsense. Rest for a quarter of an hour and then I shall be back, and this surprise will pale in comparison to that delicious meal I made you," Edrick said. Clara giggled and watched Edrick as he bid her goodbye and left the room. She was overwhelmed with emotion. Edrick had been so kind to her since her injury, first saving her, then riding to find the doctor in the middle of the night and visiting her each day. She had never had anyone but her maids cook for her, had never had someone give up time to take care of her. While she was grateful to Charity for all the care she had given her over the last few days, there was something so special about a man like Edrick, who she had previously thought so cold and closed off and unfeeling, making her meals and planning surprises for her. He really was so much more than she had originally assumed. She loved that he continued to surprise her, continued to reveal himself to her, layer by layer. He was like a puzzle, and she relished each clue he revealed to her.

Although it was true that she had felt depressed after Doctor Phillips told her she would need to stay bedridden a few more days, this day was cheering her right up.

The ride to the Morris cabin took only a few minutes, and Edrick found Jacob sitting inside, idly running his fingers through the grooves in the wooden table in the cabin's small kitchen area.

"Jacob?" Edrick called, and the boy looked up.

"Mr. Edrick! Oh, how I've missed you!" he said, sitting straight in his chair and attempting to swing his crippled leg around to stand. Edrick rushed toward him and helped him up.

"How would you like to ride with me to the ranch house to see Miss Clara?" he asked.

"Oh! Yes, please! I can show her my letters! I've been practicing them, you know. Every day, just like she told me to," Jacob said, pointing to a piece of paper on the table where Edrick could make out "My name is Jacob" and "I love to draw" written in a practiced hand.

"I can see that," Edrick said, nodding at the paper. "Well done, Jacob. She'll be very glad to hear it." They chatted for a few more minutes, and then Edrick told Jacob it was time to leave. He gently lifted Jacob and carried him out to Herbert. Jacob looked a little frightened by the horse, so Edrick showed him how to brush Herbert's flank with his hand, and the horse's tail flicked, eliciting an excited squeal from the boy.

"Do you think you're alright to sit on Herbert, Jacob? He's as gentle as they come, and we'll go real slow to the house, I promise," Edrick said, looking down at Jacob in his arms. His crippled leg meant that he couldn't stand up straight, and Edrick had thought it best to hold him while he petted Herbert, so he wouldn't get scared of the animal and accidentally trip and injure himself.

Jacob nodded. "Yes! Yes, please! Can I hold the reins?" he asked. Edrick laughed; one minute the boy was scared to touch Herbert, and the next he wanted to be the one controlling him.

"Of course you can, Jacob. I'll show you how,"

Edrick said. He hoisted Jacob onto the saddle gently, ensuring his crippled leg was tucked into the saddle so it wouldn't get jostled during the ride. Edrick got up and settled himself behind the boy, showing Jacob how to hold the saddle so he wouldn't fall.

"I've never ridden a horse before, Mr. Edrick, but I think I like it very much," Jacob said in wonder as he patted the horse's neck, rubbing his fingers through the soft, untangled mane.

"Not to worry, Jacob. I can already tell you're a natural horseman," Edrick said, and then placed one of Jacob's hands on the reins, showing him how to flick the leather straps to tell Herbert to slow down or speed up. "We're going to ride over slowly since this is your first time, okay?" Jacob looked slightly disappointed, as if he had been expecting them to set off at a fast clip, but Edrick was conscious of keeping the boy safe. Together, they signaled to Herbert to start walking, and they were off.

CHAPTER 17

Clara heard the gentle sound of horse hooves in the dirt just outside her window and was confused. The horse barn was a good few hundred feet away; there was no possible way the sound could be coming from there. So where was it coming from?

A few minutes later when Edrick walked into the room with Jacob in his arms, she found out.

"Jacob!" Clara cried, tears forming in her eyes at the sight of the boy's smiling face. "How ever did you get here?"

"I rode on a horse, Miss Clara! Mr. Edrick taught me! He says I'm a natural horseman," Jacob said, beaming. Edrick pulled a chair from one side of the room and set it next to Clara's bed and then helped Jacob settle into it.

"Oh, Jacob, you have no idea how happy I am to see you. I've missed you so," Clara said, leaning over and hugging the boy.

"I've missed you, too, Miss Clara, but I've been keeping up with our lessons. I've been practicing real hard—ask Mr. Edrick! I showed him my letters! I used the paper and pencil you gave me and everything!"

Clara looked over at Edrick who was standing in the doorway taking in the scene with a smile on his face. He had done this. He had known how much she missed Jacob, and so he had brought him to her. "Thank you," Clara mouthed to Edrick as Jacob began telling Clara the minutiae of the days they had been apart. Edrick tipped his hat in Clara's direction and left her and Jacob alone, but Clara knew she'd never be able to properly express her gratitude to Edrick, wonderful man that he was.

"I know I keep saying it but thank you so much for bringing Jacob," Clara said to Edrick a few nights after supper, while they were reading from the Bible together. After Jacob's visit, Edrick had taken to reading to Clara at night, claiming he also needed help with his reading, although she suspected it was simply an excuse to spend time with her. She was happy to play along. "You have no idea how much that visit from Jacob meant to me. I was so depressed, and seeing his smiling face, it just…"

"Brightened you right up?" Edrick said, finishing her sentence. She nodded.

"I just couldn't stand to see you so sad, Clara. A face as beautiful as yours should never have a frown on it." Clara blushed at the compliment and looked back down at the Bible in front of her. Lately, she had been blushing around Edrick more and more, at the way he spoke and the way he looked at her. Her heart and stomach fluttered every time he entered the room, and she found herself feeling bereft whenever he left her to return to the cabin.

She could feel his eyes on her now, glued to her cheeks as she pretended to read through the Book of Matthew. "Clara?" Edrick breathed from somewhere far closer to her than he had been a moment ago.

When Clara looked up, Edrick was right in front of her, his face inches from hers. "Yes?" she whispered, the word barely making a sound.

But Edrick didn't speak, he leaned closer in the chair he had placed next to her bed and placed a soft whisper of a kiss on her lips. Clara was stunned by the contact, immediately pulling away.

"I am so sorry, Clara. I don't know what came over me just now. I'll leave you be," Edrick said, rushing from his chair so quickly that it fell to the ground behind him. Clara watched him practically sprint to the door, but she called him back.

"Edrick?" He turned, looking back at her with a question in his eyes. "You did not need to apologize."

Edrick sighed with relief and nodded, seeming to understand her meaning, and then turned to leave, this time at a much slower pace. Clara sank down into the bed, still able to feel the ghost of a kiss on her lips. Her heart fluttered, there were butterflies in her stomach, and now she knew it for certain: she was in love with Edrick Ashmore.

"Another beautiful day for a walk! My, if I didn't know better, I'd say the sun has been shining extra hard just for you, Clara," Charity exclaimed a week later over breakfast.

Doctor Phillips had been to visit a few days previously and had declared Clara nearly healed. "A short walk each day, lengthening the distance by a few hundred feet each time, and I believe you shall be fully healed by Tuesday next."

Clara had nearly wept with joy at the news, glad to finally be able to move about again. Outside, spring had truly sprung, and she was itching to experience the season with her own eyes.

"Yes, well, they are much shorter than I would like my walks to be, but I suppose for now, they will have to do," Clara said, lacing her boots and giving her ankle an experimental roll. It felt stiff, but despite her long walk the day before and a bit of time in the kitchen, there was no pain. Thank goodness.

"Are you ready, Clara?" Edrick asked from the doorway. Clara stood up and nodded, and together they walked out of the house, off the porch and on towards the fields. Edrick had been the one to escort Clara on her first walk, insisting that without his presence, she was likely to attempt to traverse the whole of the ranch by herself.

"It is a truly beautiful day," Clara said, marveling at the birds singing, the sun shining and the flowers blooming on the trees planted near the fields.

"Indeed, it is, although perhaps not quite as pretty as you," Edrick said, and Clara blushed as she seemed to do so often around him.

They walked in silence a way, as had become their habit, and then began discussing life. The topic eventually turned to marriage after Edrick shared a funny story about his deceased wife and her terrible sense of direction.

"I always had to walk with her, otherwise she'd get lost and end up at the far field with the herd. The cows grew so used to her that they stopped making noises when she neared like she was an old friend."

Clara laughed, glad that Edrick felt comfortable talking about his wife. She noticed that he didn't seem sad when they spoke about her; rather, he seemed happy to reminisce about the woman he had loved. Clara hoped this meant he was finally starting to heal from all his grief and guilt.

"Clara, can I ask you something?" Edrick said, interrupting her laughter. She looked up to find him looking at her curiously. She nodded. "Why didn't you ever marry? You're smart and beautiful and well-to-do. Any man would be happy to have you for a wife."

Clara spoke without thinking. "Oh, well, I didn't feel I had met the right man." What went unsaid was that now she thought she might have.

The rest of the walk was quiet, though not with unaddressed awkwardness. Rather, both Edrick and Clara were in deep contemplation, which is why they did not hear the quick beat of hooves on the ground at that late hour, signaling that something was dreadfully wrong at the ranch house.

They were both still lost in thought as they climbed the porch steps to the main house, but then the door was flung open, and there behind Clayton was Doctor Phillips. Clara's thoughts went immediately to Charity, worried that something that happened to her cousin, but Clayton quickly disavowed her of that notion.

"It's Billy Morris. There's been an accident."

Clara and Edrick rushed into the house where Billy was lying on a blanket on the floor. His legs were bloodied, and his eyes were shut tightly, anguish clear on his face.

"What happened?" Clara whispered, turning to Charity, who was pacing nervously near the stove.

"A cattle stampede. It was completely unexpected. One of the bulls got spooked and suddenly the whole herd was charging. Billy couldn't get out of the way in time."

Clara walked over to Doctor Phillips, crouching down beside him. "Doctor? Doctor, will he heal?"

Doctor Phillips was not a man to mince words, which was why he said simply, "No."

Clara's hand flew to her mouth and tears erupted in her eyes at the thought of poor Jacob Morris experiencing another loss. She turned toward Edrick. "We must get Jacob."

Edrick turned to Clayton who was hugging Charity to his chest. The brothers nodded at each other, Clayton silently communicating that he would look after Charity and Doctor Phillips.

Clara dreaded the conversation she would have to have with Jacob, rehearsing in her head again and again what she would say to the boy, but there was precious little time to practice. Edrick had saddled Herbert and they were now flying toward the Morris cottage, Clara holding tightly to the saddle. She could feel the tension radiating off

Edrick, knowing he was feeling the same anguish as her. He had grown to care for Jacob just as much as she, and he too would be dreading telling the boy the news.

When they reached the cottage, Edrick helped Clara off the horse, and she barely had time to register his touch on her before he had taken her hand and was leading her into the house. There they found Jacob, sitting silently in front of the unlit hearth. He was writing, practicing his letters, but he looked up when Edrick and Clara walked in.

"Miss Clara? Mr. Edrick? Have you come to play?" he asked, looking at them excitedly. He hobbled to a standing position and walked toward them but stopped when he saw the tears gently sliding down Clara's face.

"Miss Clara! What's wrong?" he asked, and Clara collapsed to her knees, hugging Jacob to her chest. "Oh, Jacob, I'm so sorry, but something has happened to your father. He...he's very badly injured, and the doctor, thinks....well he thinks....that he might go to heaven."

Jacob pushed himself away from Clara's embrace, looking at her in confusion. "What do you mean? Why is he injured? Where is he? Tell me!" Suddenly, Jacob was angry, his face red and his mouth set. Clara's heart broke for him, for the poor little boy in front of her who within hours would be an orphan.

She looked up to Edrick who nodded as he lifted Jacob up. Jacob struggled, but then settled into Edrick's arms, and he carried the boy to the table, where he sat down with him in his lap. "Now, Jacob, I want you to listen to what Miss Clara has to say. We're going to make sure you're taken care of no matter what, but just at this minute, you need to listen to her. Can you do that for me?"

Jacob looked down at Edrick's arms around him and nodded, and then Clara told Jacob as calmly as possible what had happened to Billy. Jacob sniffled, then sobbed, and eventually crawled into Clara's lap, where he cried until he had no tears left in him. Then he fell asleep in her arms, and Clara hugged him close, trying to imbue him with all the love she had in her heart.

Looking outside, she realized the sun had set. "I think he needs rest, Edrick. I will take him back to the cabin with me." Edrick nodded and helped her saddle up, riding them slowly back to the ranch house. Clara couldn't face going into the main house, so she carried Jacob straight to bed, where she tucked him into Charity's vacated cot and hoped and prayed he would dream of sweet, innocent, happy moments. She suspected the news of his father to be none of those.

CHAPTER 18

Clayton, Charity, Clara and Edrick made sure that Billy Morris had a proper funeral and burial, complete with a church service attended by all the ranch hands.

The day was long and filled with sadness, and by the end Clara could see that Jacob was wilting under the weight of so much sorrow. She carried him home from the graveyard on the ranch and put him to bed, knowing he would refuse supper as he had done every night since the tragedy. "I don't want to eat unless it's with my pa," he told her each time she offered him food. When she tried to explain what had happened to Billy, Jacob lashed out, crying and screaming and breaking

Clara's heart all over again. On this day she just didn't have the energy to fight him.

Clara walked back to the main house where she saw Edrick walking up the porch steps. "Come inside and get some coffee, Clara. I suspect you could use some," he said, beckoning her inside.

Clara walked into the house to see Charity boiling water for coffee and Clayton seated at the table, his head in his hands. "What an awful day," he said, looking up and wiping his hands over his face. They all looked drawn and haggard; this was the first ranch hand death at Ashmore Ranch, and it had hit everyone hard.

Charity placed cups of coffee down in front of each of them, then took the chair across from Clayton. "Poor Jacob. To have lost both parents at such a young age…it is unimaginable."

Clayton nodded and then cleared his throat. "Yes. But while I feel for the boy, we need to decide what to do with him."

"What do you mean?" Clara asked, looking up from staring into her cup of coffee.

"Well, he is not our child. He does not belong to us, and as much as I would like to give the boy a home, I don't think it's right. If we take Jacob in, we must take every ranch hand's child in under similar circumstances, and that it is an expense and a risk I am simply not willing to take."

Clara grew angry at Clayton's brashness, not able to believe that the man she had thought so kind and loving could talk so harshly. "Clayton, be reasonable," Clara said, but Clayton shook his head.

"Clara, I know you care for the boy, but the fact of the matter is that he is not your son. Taking him in would be improper. I think it best we send him to an orphanage. They'll look after him well."

Clara could not imagine Jacob in such a place, alone, with no one to care for him, read to him, and tell him how special he was. The very thought of sending him away brought tears to her eyes. Clara looked over at Charity, who seemed ready to argue with her husband.

Edrick spoke, "Clara, would you mind accompanying me outside for a moment? There is a matter I wish to discuss with you."

Confused but too tired to argue, Clara rose and followed Edrick outside. He gestured for her to sit on one of the rocking chairs they had placed on the porch a few weeks before, when the warmth set in and the days grew longer.

"I know how angry Clayton's suggestion made

you, but I believe I have a solution that would mean Jacob wouldn't need to be sent away. He could stay right here on Ashmore Ranch."

Clara looked at Edrick questioningly and he continued. "I think that we should adopt Jacob and bring him up as our own son. He has been as good as ours for weeks now, and I would like nothing more than to bring him up as my own boy. I already love him like he is mine."

"But…but to adopt him, we would have to get married. You would have to marry me."

Edrick nodded, "Indeed." He dropped down until his right knee was touching the wood. Clara balked, confused, but then Edrick spoke, and time and noise and grief all fell away until it was just them. "Will you marry me, Clara May? I've loved you since the moment you stepped foot on this ranch, and I'd like nothing better than to make you my wife and raise Jacob as our child."

Clara's hands rose to her mouth, and for a moment she gazed at Edrick, wanting to remember that moment for the rest of time. She opened her mouth, lowered her hands, and uttered the only possible word, "Yes".

Edrick watched as Clara finished signing the

paper before her and folded it. "What was that you were writing?" he asked, sitting across from her and enjoying a rare afternoon off work. They had hired three new ranch hands and Edrick had decided to take the day off and spend it with his betrothed, reading and walking the fields hand-in-hand.

"A letter to Mr. Seymour, asking him to sell my house in New York."

Edrick sat up straight, "Are you sure? It's been your home for so long. I wouldn't begrudge you if you wanted to keep it for those rare occasions when we might go east."

Clara shook her head, "No, River Creek is my home now, the only home I'll ever need." Clara looked up and met Edrick's eyes, and they shared a private gaze filled with love and friendship, a gaze they shared often in the years that followed.

CHAPTER 19

"I can't believe we're both married," Clara said to Charity as they walked the fields one afternoon. Her and Edrick's wedding had taken place the week previously, a small ceremony with just the couple, Charity, Clayton and Jacob present.

Jacob was still wracked with grief over his father's death but had been overjoyed at the news that Clara and Edrick were getting married, exclaiming "Finally!" when they told him. Apparently, he had noticed their connection before either of them had acknowledged it.

"Married, and you with a son. My, how things have changed since we set foot here a few months ago." Charity nodded, thinking of Jacob back in the house with Edrick. They had taken over the back cabin, altering it slightly so Jacob had his own room. Clara spent much of her day teaching him, and the rest playing with him, until Edrick came home. Then they ate together, read more, and talked. They were all still adjusting to each other, to their newfound bond as a family. Just the night before, Jacob told Clara he loved her when she kissed him goodnight, and her heart had sung. She had more than she could have ever dreamed of, and she had Charity to thank.

"It's all because of you, Charity. If you hadn't told me you were coming here alone, I never would have accompanied and I wouldn't have any of this," she said, gesturing to Edrick and Jacob on horseback in the pasture beside them where Edrick was helping Jacob learn to canter.

"Do you recall that you told me that certain danger awaited me in the Wild West, danger you needed to protect me from," Charity said with a huge smile on her face.

Clara laughed. "Yes, well, whatever version of events you want to believe, I'm still happy I came. I'm so happy," she said, turning to look at her husband and son.

"Do you not think Jacob will get lonely, being the only child in the family?"

Charity asked Clara as they watched the boys laughing and feeding Herbert an old apple.

"I don't think so, no. Why, do you think he will?" Clara asked, turning to her cousin.

Charity shrugged. "I doubt it, now that he has a cousin on the way," she said, patting her belly. Clara's eyes widened with recognition, and then she squealed and hugged Charity close, tears of pure joy springing in her eyes at the good fortune that River Creek had brought them both.

GET A FREE BOOK

Click below to download this story for free.

The Texan Rancher's Bride

HAVE YOU READ?

When tragedy strikes, can a mail order bride find love and uncover a hidden truth in the wilds of Montana?

Whispers of the West

Desperate and alone, Sarah Wilkins is stripped of all she holds dear when a merciless illness claims her parents. With no job or home, she teeters on the brink of giving up—until the Matrimonial Times offers her a glimmer of hope.

Dreaming of a fresh start in the West, Sarah corresponds with three suitors. After they disappoint her, a friend's encouragement leads her to find new hope with Tom Dean in Montana's wilds.

However, fate has other plans for Sarah. When she arrives in Montana, her anticipated future slips from her grasp once more. Taken in by the Dean family, she forms close bonds with Tom's siblings, Cathy, Molly, Jack, and Ben.

Yet, an unsettling mystery looms over the ranch as cattle begin to vanish, and Sarah is determined to unveil the truth whatever the cost may be.

Embark on a captivating journey through the heart of the West in this enthralling mail order bride romance. Amidst the beauty of prairie sunsets, Sarah navigates a path riddled with unexpected challenges and revelations.

Made in the USA
Middletown, DE
02 December 2024

65926454R00110